The Christmas City Vampire

By Larry L. Deibert

Dedication

Peggy, you are my wife and my best friend. This book never would have been written without your encouragement.

Friday, November 26th, 2010

Black Friday was over. The traditional first day of the Christmas season, as far as merchants were concerned, was a glorious day for Jenna Blackman as she counted the cash receipts and checks in her nearly overflowing register drawer. Ten minutes later, she finished the count, entered the amount on her spreadsheet, and saw that her store, Cozy Capers, in downtown Bethlehem, Pa., had shown a profit of $3,221.17. *Not bad for a weak economy,* she thought.

Jenna put the cash and checks into a bank bag, turned off the lights and locked the front door behind her. It had begun to snow around three-thirty, which might have kept some shoppers away, but all in all it had been a fantastic day. As she began the three-block walk to her car, she cautiously looked at the pedestrians still walking up and down Main Street. She saw a cop up the street, and that gave her some sense of security. He was only a block or so from where her car was parked on a side street. Normally, her husband Jim would be walking with her but he had felt ill, earlier in the day, so she had made him go home to lie down and take it easy.

As she passed the door of an Italian restaurant, two patrons strolled out. She caught a whiff of the food that was being prepared inside. Her stomach started rumbling; she had been too busy all day to eat, except for a hasty breakfast of half of a toasted bagel with cream cheese and a cup of coffee. She considered calling Jim on her cell to see if he wanted her to pick up something for dinner, but making a meal was the last thing on her mind. She would much rather just take a load off her feet and enjoy a glass or two of wine before crawling into bed. She hoped that tomorrow would be another good day in the store, but if the snow kept up, her profits from today could just as easily be negated.

As Jenna turned the corner at the mouth of the side street, she slipped, dropping the money bag as she fell hard on her chest. Stunned, she began to cry. Then she heard a man say, "Looks like you took a nasty spill. Here, take my hand and I'll help you up. Is your car nearby?"

When she was back on her feet, she smiled, recognizing her white knight as someone who had spent quite a bit of money, earlier, in her store. "Thanks, but I dropped my bank bag and I need to find it."

"Good day at the store?"

"Better than good. It was the best day we ever had. People were buying everything and I was busy as hell from opening to close. You certainly helped a lot with my day."

"That's good to know. I think all the merchants did pretty well. I've been in town most of the day, visiting the shops and eateries, and all the owners had smiles on their faces. This might be Bethlehem's best Christmas in years." He looked around, scanning the area. "Accuweather said we could get up to six inches before tomorrow afternoon, but I think people will still come out and – Ah!" He picked up the bag and handed it to her.

"Thanks."

"Not at all. Would you like me to escort you to your car?"

"Yes, I'd like that. Thank you so much."

They walked side by side, casually talking as a car came down the narrow street a little too fast and nearly slid into them.

Jenna gave the kid the finger and yelled a couple of profane words, but the kid just gave them the finger back and kept on going without even an "I'm sorry."

Jenna shook her head. "There are kids driving cars today that shouldn't even be allowed to ride a bike, and all the college kids drinking and carousing till all hours. I guess I shouldn't worry so much but, since we lost Dan, I get testy real easy."

"Who's Dan?"

"Dan was our son. He was hit by a car a couple of years ago. Cops never caught the guy, but I'm pretty sure it was someone Jim and I knew. I just don't think I can ever prove it." She grew quiet.

"I'm so sorry. How old would he be now?"

"Ten." She looked toward her escort. "It was rough, having a baby at twenty, but Jim and I were so much in love that we were able to provide for Dan, even though we were still in school." She fell silent again until they reached her car. "Well, here we are." She took out her keys, unlocked the door and opened it. Jenna threw her purse and the bank bag on the back seat, then turned to thank her escort

Instead, her mouth opened and she drew breath to scream at the sight of his face, which had transformed into a mask of pure evil. His strong right hand closed over her mouth as two sharp teeth pierced her neck. Jenna struggled, but the blood was sucked from her at such a rapid rate that she lost consciousness and slid, unresisting, into death.

When the vampire had finished, he laid her body gently on the snow-covered street. "I'm so sorry, Jenna, but I couldn't wait any longer. It had to be you."

"Hey!" someone yelled from behind him. "What are you doing?"

One furtive glance was enough to identify the man as a cop. Although the snow was bound to shroud his visibility, the vampire did not intend to give him a chance at a better look, and took off, much faster than humanly possible

It only took the cop thirty seconds to race up the alley, but the man was already out of sight. He looked down at the woman, and saw the twin wounds on her neck, and the way her sightless eyes stared vacantly upward.

With a shudder, he called the station.

Two blocks away, fifteen yards deep into an alley strewn with snow-covered black plastic bags that reeked of garbage, the vampire found a large shard of a broken mirror and held it up. Seeing no blood splatter, he nodded, satisfied, and strolled out of the alley.

****

Corporal Michael McGinnis stood at the scene of the murder for nearly fifteen minutes, waiting for a detective to arrive. Someone from the coroner's office would probably arrive within a few minutes to a half hour depending on the worsening driving conditions.

As he waited, McGinnis, a seven-year veteran of the BPD, kept glancing at the body lying near his feet. Jenna Blackman had been a beautiful woman. Statuesque at five feet nine inches tall, she had long, auburn hair, hazel eyes, and a smile that radiated joy all the time. He and his wife, Jean, were friends of the Blackmans, and he knew Jim would take the news of his wife's death hard. Although soft-spoken, she could become animated and quite vocal when she chatted about anything she had a passion for. Jenna loved to paint and some her work was displayed on the walls of her shop, but she never had the desire to part with any, no matter how much was offered. She had known most of her customers, and addressed many of them by their first names.

He raised his eyes to the darkness above, offering a short prayer, then looked back down at the body. Her long legs, one bent over the other, were covered by black woolen slacks. She wore a mid-length red coat, and her hands were inside cream-colored wool gloves. The lipstick she wore looked even more pronounced because of her stone-white face, totally devoid of blood. Tears formed, and Mike wiped them away with a gloved hand, just as a detective arrived at the scene.

The detective stuck out his hand and introduced himself. "Corporal McGinnis? I'm Detective Hyram Lasky. Are you the officer who reported the homicide?"

"Yes, sir, I am." Out of long-standing habit, McGinnis found himself studying Lasky for a moment. He stood about five feet nine inches tall, probably weighed one seventy or so, and he was wearing a charcoal overcoat. The detective had dark brown hair, with a few wisps of gray over his ears, a classic Roman nose and dark, brown eyes. Lasky flashed a smile filled with slightly yellowing teeth.

The detective put on a pair of latex gloves and squatted down beside the body to measure the distance between the two wounds on her neck with his pen. "All right, McGinnis, tell me what you saw." He stood up and walked to the car. The driver's door was still open, a purse and a bank bag clearly visible in the back seat.

"I saw this lady. Jenna Blackman. She and her husband Jim own Cozy Capers on Main Street. Anyway, I saw Mrs. Blackman walking up Main, but when she rounded the corner, she slipped on the snow and took a nasty spill. I headed her way, but a man was already coming to her aid."

"Did you get a good look at him?" Lasky opened the purse and glanced at the driver's license, credit cards and cash. The bank bag was filled with checks and paper currency, eliminating robbery as a motive. Frowning, he bagged it all, then bent to look at the body.

"No sir. I know he had a goatee and mustache and he was wearing glasses, but he turned away too quickly for me to recognize him. He wore black pants, a black jacket, and a black watch cap, but that's about all I got."

Lasky nodded and stood up. "So, what happened next?" He took out a cigarette, lit it, and offered one to McGinnis.

The officer accepted, lit up and blew out a plume of smoke. "Well, sir, it looked to me like she knew him. When they started to walk up the alley, I figured she was okay and didn't require my assistance. A short time later, walking my beat, I looked up the alley and saw a man – the same man, I think – kneeling beside Mrs. Blackman. She was laying face-up. The man glanced my way, but I still couldn't get a good look at his face. The snow was coming down hard, by then." McGinnis took a deep drag of his cigarette and blew out the smoke, clearly shaken. "I ran up the alley, but the man got up and disappeared. I tell you, Detective; I've never seen anyone move so quickly. I knew I wouldn't be able to catch him, so I checked on Mrs. Blackman. When I bent down to feel for a pulse, I saw the wounds on her neck, but there was no blood. Not a drop. And look at how white her face is, like the blood was completely drained from her. I don't believe in fairy tales or things that go bump in the night, but I'd say whatever killed her wasn't human. I hate to say it, sir, but she looks like she was killed by a vampire."

Lasky put his hands on his hips and laughed. "Seriously, McGinnis? Come on, you don't really believe in that crap, do you?"

McGinnis shrugged defensively. "Well, how would you explain it? One minute, he was poised over her body, and the next he was running off, faster than humanly possible. She has two wounds on her neck and her body is devoid of blood. What am I supposed to think?"

"Maybe the woman was attacked by a large dog, and the man was trying to help her out."

"Then why run away, sir?"

"That's a good question... Ah. The coroner's here. We'll know more once the body's been examined." He put his hand on McGinnis's shoulder. "Why don't you head back to the station and write your report? If I find anything out, I'll give you a call. We can discuss it over a beer."

"Okay, sir. I'll call a patrol to take me in." He handed Lasky a card. "Here's my home and cell numbers."

Watching him go, Lasky put the card in his wallet, then waited while the body was loaded into the coroner's van before he finally felt free to hop into his car and leave the scene.

****

Lasky was in the shower when the phone began to ring. Cursing, he threw back the shower curtain and snatched up the phone. "Lasky."

"Hyram, this is Everett Gardner from the coroner's office. How are you this evening?"

"Great, Everett, but can I call you back in a few minutes. I was in the shower, and I'm standing in a puddle on my bathroom floor."

"Certainly. Take your time. This body isn't going anywhere." He emitted a bark of laughter and hung up the phone.

Lasky stepped back into the shower and finished washing himself. Murders always made him feel extra dirty, so he languished for a few more minutes before stepping out to towel off.

He strolled to the kitchen and grabbed a beer, then headed into the living room. Settling down in a comfortable chair, he opened the bottle of Yuengling, took a deep pull, set the bottle down, and punched in the numbers on his phone.

"Coroner's Office, Gardner speaking."

Ev, its Hy." He reached for the bottle. "What ya got for me?"

Everett replied, "Mrs. Blackman was bitten by something. If I were a betting man, I'd say that her wounds were caused by something similar to canine teeth. The skin around the wounds was upraised, leading me to believe that, when she was attacked, whatever did it was sucking hard. Blood loss was significant. Her body contained less than a half a pint, so I'm estimating that whatever did this drained around three and a half quarts of blood, judging by Mrs. Blackman's height and weight. I don't know of any animal indigenous to this area that's strong or quick enough to do that kind of damage, especially not in what was probably less than five minutes, based on the account you gave me."

"So, what does your gut tell you, Ev?"

"Good question. I'd say she was killed by something that wasn't human *or* animal. Maybe a hybrid that escaped from some top-secret government facility? My best guess would be that she was killed by a vampire-like creature, except no such creatures exist. What do you think?"

Hyram took a final pull of his beer, shaking his head. "I honestly have no idea, but Corporal McGinnis seems to agree with your theory. I think I'm going to have to see what he actually knows about vampires. I can't believe I'm saying that, but we have nothing else to go on. Talk to you later."

"Take care, Hy. Say hello to Lucy for me."

"Will do. Bye." He hung up the phone, pulled McGinnis's card from his wallet, and dialed the home number. When McGinnis answered he said, "Corporal, could you meet me at Westy's Bar and Grill in about half an hour?"

"Certainly, Detective. See you there."

Saturday, November 27th, 2010

As the news of Jenna Blackman's murder spread, people who would normally have gone about their business stayed at home, glued to the TV, or surfed the Internet for more information. Coerced by snow and fear, several shopkeepers decided to close temporarily, forgoing what would have been a heavy shopping day.

Jim Blackman unlocked the door to Cozy Capers and walked in. Tired of the corporate life, he and Jenna had leased the store almost four years ago, determined to have their own business. Jim had a nice nest egg from his grandparent's estate, so the rent was affordable, and they reasoned that they would be fine for a few years, even if they made no money.

When the door opened, he could immediately smell her perfume even through all the particular scents of candles and potpourri. She was as much of a fixture in that place as the lights, the walls, and floor and all the merchandise that would never be touched by her again. Jim thought he had cried himself out after the police officers gave him the news, but he now knew that the crying might never end. It was going to be a difficult time, allowing the investigators to dust everything in the store for prints and sit down with him to watch the security camera tapes from yesterday. She'd be in a lot of the frames, laughing and smiling with her customers. God, how that woman could smile and laugh. His heart was aching, but he wanted the bastard that killed her to be caught. Actually, he wanted to strangle him, but his hands were so shaky, he didn't know if they'd ever work right again.

A team of police officers and detectives arrived a few minutes behind him and set up a yellow Do Not Cross tape barricade strung from both sides of the building out to the street. Local store owners and curiosity seekers gathered beyond the makeshift barricade, their numbers increasing until traffic was impeded and more police officers had to be summoned to the scene to restore control.

Jim had stepped outside before everyone was dispersed and spoke, in a voice choked with emotion. "Thank you for stopping by, and for the calls on the answering machine, both at home and here at the store. I can't say much, but rest assured I fully expect the

Bethlehem Police Department to find the man who committed this crime." At that, he broke down and stepped back inside.

As they viewed the tapes, Detective Lasky saw himself chatting with Jenna yesterday morning.

"You were here, yesterday, Lasky?" asked Detective Miles Steele.

"Yeah, Miles. I try to visit businesses wherever I am, just to see if everyone is doing okay. Been doing that for as long as I can remember, even when I was a cop in Ohio."

Miles nodded as they continued to view the tapes, fast forwarding when needed. The last thing they saw was Jenna reaching down behind the counter to turn off the camera before leaving for the day.

"I'm sorry, Jim, but I don't see anything or anyone suspicious. I'm going to have the guys stop dusting because I don't think we'll come up with anything, since the majority of visitors to the store today were definitely shoppers. There were only a dozen or so men inside the store all day. Two of them more or less fit the description, but chances are they were from out of town."

"Thanks, Detective Steele. Honestly, I've had enough time here today myself. Will we really find this guy, or is my wife going to be another stat?"

"I hope not, Mr. Blackman, but we don't really have anything yet, and none of the people we canvassed had anything to offer. But we'll keep working on this case until we find your wife's murderer or they pull the plug on us."

Jim Blackman simply nodded. Soon after the team removed the yellow tape barrier, he closed the doors, wondering if he would ever be able to reopen.

****

Later that day, although Lasky, McGinnis and Gardner didn't know how, the word 'vampire' leaked to the news services.

Sunday, November 28th, 2010

Despite seeing the story on TV, or reading about it in the morning paper, more and more local residents were beginning to venture outside again. There was still a gripping fear that any one of them might be the vampire's next victim, but the need to bond with other humans far outweighed the terror that they felt.

Churches filled, their collection plates overflowing. After services concluded, people went about their usual Sunday agendas by going to diners and restaurants for breakfast, brunch or early lunches, depending on the times of the services.

Stores opened, and nothing deterred people from their shopping excursions. Those stores that hadn't mailed out a flyer or taken an ad in the newspapers hung hand-made signs on their doors, offering savings up to seventy percent. How could people even consider staying home when they could save so much money during the Christmas shopping season? Patrons may have figured that, since they had just devoted an hour or two to God, they would be safe to gather without having to worry about a blood-sucking killer vampire walking the streets of their city. Those shoppers who were more timid chose to go to places like the Whitehall and Lehigh Valley Malls or the Promenade Shops in Saucon Valley. Many stores posted pictures of the two men from the Cozy Capers security cameras, asking anyone who recognized one or both of the men to contact the Bethlehem Police Department immediately.

Later that afternoon, Mike arrived with his partner, Sara Jameison, and was surprised by the change that had occurred since Jenna's murder. . He felt a little more bullet proof than the day before, but he knew it was a temporary stopgap, at best.

"Sara, this mood swing really bothers me. Last night was pretty dead. We're a strange breed sometimes."

"What do you mean?"

"Well, here we are, with a mythical creature who killed one of our best-liked store owners, less than forty-eight hours ago, and yet life seems to have gotten back to normal, even though the threat is still out there." He turned toward her. "Do you remember what you felt like when the planes hit the towers and the Pentagon?"

"Yes, I do," she replied in a somber tone. "I lost a good friend at the Pentagon, and I was ready to sign on the dotted line and go to war because of what those people did."

"Okay, but you didn't. I know you will never forget your friend, but once your anger subsided, you got on with your life, even though we know that the terrorist community is not finished with us yet. We let our guard down and, bang, we were in a mini-shitstorm." He sighed, not wanting to lose control of his emotions.

She touched his shoulder. "You don't have to talk about it if you don't want to say any more."

"Thanks, but I just needed a moment there. I remember all the flags that were put out in front of nearly everyone's home, but over a period of time, they became forgotten pieces of cloth, torn and faded because people had more important things to focus on. People started going to church again, like they have today, but how long will that last?

"Sara, we became so enraged with all the Muslims in the world, like it was their fault because a few people of Muslim heritage shocked the world with what they did, and I guess there are still a huge number of people that will feel that way until they die

"When the planes hit, that day, a Vietnam vet friend of mine was out in Kokomo, Indiana, at a huge Vietnam veteran reunion that culminated on the following Sunday, which was National POW-MIA Day. Anyway, when they watched the events unfolding and the second plane hit, he became extremely bitter toward the 'ragheads,' as the vets referred to the terrorists. When the Pentagon was hit, the frustration and anger of those vets mushroomed to a point where they were ready to put their gear back on and 'wipe all them motherfuckers off the face of the earth.'

"My friend, who hadn't had a cigarette in almost nineteen years, began smoking again. His nerves were shot. He went to a candlelight vigil that night, and to an army buddy's church the next day. It was then he remembered that he had a good friend back here who happened to be a Muslim married to a Christian. Deep inside, he knew that the blame shouldn't fall on a whole nation, just on the people and terrorist group that were responsible.

"I guess what I'm trying to say is that we forget quickly, and keep on keeping on with our lives."

Sara sat quietly for a minute, and sighed. "True. I guess it's human nature. We realize there isn't much we can do, especially in a situation like this. We don't even know how or if this thing can be killed. Will a stake to the heart do it? Will Jenna Blackman rise someday as a vampire and start her own reign of terror? Are there more vampires out there? The way I look at it, all we can do is go on with our lives and deal with terrorists, vampires, and whatever else might plague us when it happens. You know how it is, Mike. We wear uniforms and badges, and we carry guns, because it's our job to protect people as best we can. But we can talk till we're blue in the face without changing people's minds about how they feel or what they're going to do in any given situation."

Mike nodded. Then, spotting an accident involving three cars up ahead, he toggled the lights and sirens.

Monday, November 29th, 2010

Michael McGinnis studied his face in the mirror. At thirty-two, he sometimes felt much older. His dark brown hair was beginning to speckle with gray. His brown eyes were a little sunken, and he was starting to sport small bags beneath them. He had lost a couple of pounds in the past six months, mostly in his face, making it look more elongated. Mike always felt tired, no matter how much rest he got. The job was definitely getting to him, and he truly wondered if he would be able to complete a thirty-year career as a police officer. With budget cuts around every corner, and an economy that didn't look likely to get much better in the near future, he had begun to consider moonlighting as a security guard. He knew a couple of guys on the force who worked security, and some of the money was under the table. *Screw the taxman*, he thought. He already paid enough. Jean was always bugging him about looking for a bigger house—she wanted four bedrooms, but Michael thought three was plenty since they didn't plan on having kids.

He shook off the depressing thoughts and concentrated on shaving. According to the clock above the toilet, he needed to put the pedal to the metal if he was going to report for work in less than a half hour.

By the time he drove to the station, his thoughts were circling Jenna's murder again. The autopsy had revealed nothing about whether her attacker was animal or human. The only given was that the body was nearly drained of blood – nearly ninety-five percent blood loss. On Friday night, Detective Lasky had laughed when the word *vampire* was mentioned, but now the word had come down that he wanted to know all the old wives' tales and mythology about that kind of a creature, especially what could supposedly kill one. *Why the hell does he want to know all that, if there's no such thing on this earth?* McGinnis pondered, then shook his head as he realized that he was pulling into the BPD parking lot without the least memory of having driven there.

****

Letter carrier Brian Miller was completely disgusted as he turned off the light at his mailman case. He had hoped to work only an eight-hour day, but that wasn't happening, due to the amount of delayed mail piled on the floor, early Christmas packages out the ying-yang, and an hour and a half wait for the DPS mail to arrive from the facility on Route 512. When he punched out, the time read 5:20. Ten more minutes and he would have had ten hours. Sure, the OT money really helped out, especially since The Sands built that money-sucking casino a couple of minutes' drive down the road. He'd been addicted from the moment he stepped inside for the first time. Over the years, Atlantic City and the occasional poker game with his letter-carrier buddies had bled a few hundred bucks from him, but now he could go over damn near any time he wanted, since the place was directly on his way home to Hellertown.

As soon as he stepped outside, he was once again chilled to the bone. That was the bad thing about the ten minutes or so he'd spent inside the warm Post Office. Park-and-loop routes like his offered little to keep a man warm on a cold day. Park the truck, deliver to as many as fifty houses, then climb back inside the freezer on wheels to move, what, a whole couple of blocks to park and walk all over again. People always thought the mailman had a good job, but no one ever wanted to trade places on days like this, only during the spring and fall when the weather was nearly perfect. *Oh well. Twenty-five more years and I can pack it in*, he thought as he opened his car door.

When Brian went to start up the car, the engine wouldn't even try to turn over. Belatedly, he noticed that the headlight switch was in the 'on' position, and he slammed the steering wheel with his gloved hand. "What the hell else can go wrong today?"

He exited the car and looked around for someone who could give him a jump, but nobody was in sight. He pulled out his cell phone, and a sardonic smile crossed his face: no freaking service! "How in the hell can I be in a highly populated area and not have any service?" He muttered out loud.

Brian bundled himself inside his winter uniform jacket. If he started walking toward The Sands, maybe he'd be able to hitch a ride. Even if he couldn't, he'd be able to get some hot food and a few cold ones once he got there. With everything that had gone wrong, maybe tonight Lady Luck would shine down on him and he'd win enough to buy a new car instead of his twelve-year-old piece-of-shit Toyota. *You just never know,* he thought as he started walking toward the bright lights at The Sands.

****

Earlier, McGinnis and Jameison got a call to investigate a disturbance outside the Bethlehem Brew Works. When they arrived on the scene, two young, possibly underage white kids were visibly drunk as they tried to gain entrance to the popular drinking spot.

The officers checked their ID cards, but they didn't really want to take the young man and woman downtown. The kids had clearly had a couple more than they should have, but their Pennsylvania driver's licenses showed that they were both over twenty-one. Although by only four days, the twins were legal. One of the staff members commented that the two kids weren't really too bad; they had just been egged on by some of their friends. "I know them both, and they really are good kids. Can you give them a break?"

Jameison, who was definitely more than attracted to the female staff member, answered, "No problem. McGinnis and I will just release them to their folks with a little pep talk." She smiled brightly and the staff member, Gloria Knecht, caught on immediately.

"Thanks, guys. Listen, I gotta go home for awhile, but I should be here later if you feel like having a drink after work?"

"That'd be cool. I think I can make it, but Mike probably has to go home to the ball and chain. He has a short leash on school nights. Don't you, Mikey?"

McGinnis knew exactly what was going on, so he replied. "Yeah, Gloria, she's right. I generally don't hang out after work unless I'm off the next day, so I'll take a rain check."

Back in the car, Sara, said, "Thanks. She's really hot and maybe – just maybe – the two of us can get something going."

He nodded. "It's cool, as long as you never tell me about the sex." He laughed and she laughed along with him as the two passengers in the back seat were totally lights out.

****

Brian Miller had been on foot for less than ten minutes when he heard a car horn behind him. He turned toward the sound as a car pulled up beside him. A husky voice from inside called out, "Need a lift?"

"Thanks!" Brian said, the word carried along on his visible breath. Hopping into the car, which was toasty warm, he took off his gloves.

"Where ya headed to, my friend?"

He pulled his bottle of water from his coat pocket and took a quick pull before replying, "I was going to go to The Sands and win some money, but if you wouldn't mind dropping me at home instead, I'd really appreciate it."

"Sure. Where's home?"

"Society Hill. The condo complex just outside of Hellertown."

"Can do. Are you feeling any warmer?"

"Yeah, I am. Mind if I smoke?" He looked toward the driver but really couldn't get a good look at him. The dome light was out and he had the hood of his sweatshirt pulled forward around his face.

"No, I don't mind. As a matter a fact, I was going to have one, too." He lit up and took a drag. "So, how come you're walking home? I'm gonna make a wild guess that you left the Post Office not too long ago."

"What gave me away?" He laughed, knowing an old mailman joke was probably going to be uttered any second. He had heard them all, but he was willing to play nice with the guy for giving him a ride.

The man glanced toward him and said, in an apologetic tone, "I didn't mean to insult you for being a mailman. In fact I have great respect for what you and your co-workers do, delivering mail six days a week in all kinds of weather. Certainly not a job I'd like to have."

Brian was shocked that this guy wasn't going to crack any jokes about the service, and that he seemed to really appreciate what a carrier did every day. "Thanks, buddy. We don't hear that too often. I appreciate the compliment."

"Well, I know where you're coming from. I have a few friends who work for the Postal Service on both sides of the fence. Gotta tell ya, with everything I've heard, that's the most mismanaged place on the face of the earth. I hope it survives so everyone can retire and have a good life down the road."

The rest of the trip was made in silence, as Brian drifted to sleep.

In less than a half hour, he was taking a hot shower, after which he headed straight to bed. The Sands would have to wait until another day.

****

After Mike and Sara dropped the twins off and had a talk with their parents, they returned to their routine patrol. Eight inches of snow in the past four days was a lot for that early in the season, but with all the Christmas lights reflecting a multitude of colors off the pure white, the city of Bethlehem was prettier still.

Settled by the Moravians back in 1741, it still retained a number of its original and fully restored buildings, and the famous Bethlehem street lamps gave Main Street an antiquated but charming appearance. Many of the shops and restaurants had been in business for a long time. Up on the mountain, the Star of Bethlehem came to life every night and could be seen from a great distance, much like the real star that hovered over a manger over two-thousand years earlier. In 1937, the Bethlehem Chamber of Commerce began promoting the city as the Christmas City. Since then, Bethlehem had gained worldwide fame as Christmas City, USA.

As they cruised, they scanned closed stores and noted that the restaurants weren't as busy as usual, because of the weather, but that the Bethlehem Brew Works and most of the bars they passed were hopping. Somehow, lousy weather always brought more people out.

At a crosswalk, they stopped the car, waiting for a couple to cross. The man was very tall, dressed in a sweatshirt, and the tiny woman by his side was wearing a short skirt and boots. They nodded as they crossed the street, holding hands.

McGinnis thought he recognized the guy as the drummer from a band he had followed, several years ago. He'd have to check out his CDs to see if he was right.

"Mike, I'm hungry. Can we take a break? And I really have to pee."

Mike frowned as he shot her a glance. "TMI, partner." Then he smiled and looked at his watch, which read 9:15. "Sure. Eat at the Brew Works?"

"You read my mind, partner."

"Maybe we can even hang out for a little while. It's been a pretty quiet shift so far."

Mike grabbed a table and sat down while Sara made her way to the bathroom. Gloria looked their way and quickly made a beeline for the bathroom, as well. Mike saw her catch up with Sara and when it looked as if she was going to grab her ass, he turned away. He had a lot of gay friends, but he sure as hell didn't need to see what they did behind – no, sometimes not even behind – closed doors. He never thought for a minute in the two years that he'd known Sara that she might be gay. Hell, when things weren't going well with the wife, and it seemed like she might toss him out because of the job and money stress and too much booze, he'd figured he'd see if he and Sara might hook up. He smiled inwardly. Clearly, that stood all the chance of the proverbial snowball in hell.

A man came over to the table and caught Mike's attention. "My name is Bruce and I'll be your server tonight. Would you like something to drink?"

"Hi, Bruce. My partner and I each need a cup of coffee. Then she'd like the Slag Pot Meatloaf and I'd like the Steelgaarden Salad with Balsamic Vinaigrette. I guess one of your servers, Gloria Knecht, will be joining us, so add her order to my bill."

"That'll be great, Officer McGinnis," the man said, reading his nametag. "I'll be right back with your coffee."

While Mike waited for Sara and Gloria to finish doing God knew what, he scoped out the bar, as any good cop would do.

The place was pretty full, even though it was only Monday night. Lots of people were out of work but they still managed to come up with enough money to drown their troubles here. College kids of both sexes used the bar as their sexual chessboard, making moves, taking out pawns with looks of disdain, marching back and forth on the board until they found their king or queen for the night, or the week, or longer. He had a friend, who'd met a guy at a bar when she got stood up by a blind date. That one had worked out; they lived together for nearly ten years and finally getting hitched in August, with a nice wedding at Jacobsburg Park...

"Hi, Mike. Sorry we kept you waiting."

Mike snapped out of his waking coma and smiled at Gloria. "That's okay. I was in one of those zones and didn't hear you guys sit down." She was a nice-looking woman, dressed in tight jeans and a T-shirt. Her boobs were a little small, but other than that, she was pretty well-built. Her short, black hair was nicely groomed, and her face was pretty.

Sara looked at her partner, worry lines creasing her brow. "You okay? You can't zone out when you're on the job, Mike, even on a break."

He shot her a look. "You know, if I were a writer, I could kill you off like this." He snapped his fingers, just as Bruce arrived with the drinks.

After some lively conversation, and the consumption of their food, Gloria inquired about the murder. "Any leads on Jenna's killer? I really liked her a lot."

"No, we don't know any more than you do," Sara replied.

"It's so sad, and all this vampire talk scares the hell out of me."

"We were talking about that yesterday. Some kind of whack job kills a local, and people are scared, thinking they're going to be next. Maybe it's a one-and-done job. We can only hope."

Once they were back out on the street, Sara squeezed his arm. Thanks. "This job can play hell on relationships. I guess I'm trying to say that, even though we are miles apart sexually, I'll always have your back out here on the street."

Before Mike had a chance to respond, the radio crackled to life. "Unit Seven, respond to a disturbance in the apartment building above the Wired Café. A homeless woman made her bed on the mail counter in the vestibule and she needs to be escorted from the building. She won't leave on her own."

Sara keyed the mic. "Roger that. ETA in two." She looked at Mike. "Full moon?"

They both laughed, knowing the full moon was a week past, but whatever tension there had been from their dinner evaporated. They were back to being cops again.

****

Detective Hyram Lasky was growing increasingly preoccupied with the investigation of Jenna Blackman's death. He pulled up all reports written up by Corporal McGinnis, the team of detectives, and the police officers who canvassed all the businesses on Main Street. Residents of the apartments had also been questioned, to see if anyone had seen the man who helped Jenna when she slipped and fell, but no significant information had been uncovered. One hidden security camera recorded the man and Jenna together as they walked a short distance up the side street, but they soon passed out of view. The man's identity was still a mystery and likely to remain that way, since they knew nothing beyond his estimated height, and a generic description of dark trousers and shoes or overshoes, a black coat and gloves. They were no closer to getting any kind of ID on him, even after some of the most promising frames were enhanced.

Detective Frank Beck handed him a cup of coffee. "Hy, I think you need to take off and get a little rest. This case is staring to beat you up already."

He lifted the cup to his lips and took a sip. "Thanks, Frank, but there has to be something from this video recording, or maybe someone saw the guy and hasn't come forward yet." He leaned back in his chair. "You head on home. I'm gonna keep working for a while, and then head back to the scene and look around. Maybe I'll get lucky and run into someone who saw something. Jenna was good people. She didn't deserve to die like that."

"Okay, man, but if you get into a tight spot, give someone here a holler."

"Will do. Can ya tell me who's patrolling in that area tonight?"

Frank picked up a roster from his desk and scanned the patrol pairings. "McGinnis and Jameison."

"Thanks, pal. Now get your ass home before your old lady thinks you're doing something ya shouldn't be doing."

****

The seven-story parking deck at The Sands was pretty full for late on a Monday night. Late hours and bad weather never kept the gamblers away.

After finding a spot on the fifth deck, he took the elevator down to the first floor. The bright lights and noise inside the casino were daunting, but the vampire intended to find a suitable victim for tonight.

He sat down at a dollar machine and started playing. Touching the front of the machine each time he pressed the button, he could tell when it was time to play the maximum bet-three dollars. His amazing sense of touch never let him down. He pressed 'Max Bet' and was rewarded with a five-hundred-dollar hit. He pressed 'Cash Out,' grabbed his voucher and headed to the redemption machine, where he received five crisp one-hundred-dollar bills. He made a point of never applying for a casino card; he certainly didn't need another system to have all his information and his picture. Recognition was one thing he definitely did not need. He had had quite enough of that in the last one hundred and fifty years.

Moving on to a quarter machine, he sat three seats away from a beautiful young woman who seemed a little down. After only five minutes of playing, she fed the machine a fifty dollar bill, started playing 'Max Bet,' and was down to a few bucks in no time. Another fifty went into the slot.

The vampire cashed out and took a seat beside her. He played two or three times, then said out loud, "Okay you one-armed bastard, I'm playing a 'Max Bet,' and ya better pay off." He pressed the button and was rewarded with a four-hundred-dollar hit.

The woman, appearing impressed, leaned toward him. "Can you rub some of your luck on my machine? I'm down over a deuce and I surely can't afford it, but I can't stay away from this place."

He smiled. "Tell ya what. You just play, betting one or two, and I'll let ya know when to shoot the moon. If ya win, buy me a drink. How's that sound?"

She gave him a look, as if unsure whether she should really put any stock into what he offered, but she wasn't doing anything on her own, and he seemed to be doing pretty damn well.

"Okay, mister, let's give it a shot." She bet two and got nothing, then bet one and busted again. Next, she played two and hit a couple of bucks. "So, when is your magic going to do its thing?" She looked to him for guidance, and he held up five fingers. She pressed five and spun the wheels.

The bonus section lit up.

He told her which boxes to press.

When all was said and done, she was up three-hundred-seventy dollars.

"Wow that was cool! Can I win some more?"

He nodded, and she continued to look to him for instructions.

After ten minutes, she was down to a little over a hundred bucks, clearly sorry that she hadn't cashed out, bought him a drink and been done with it.

He put his hand on her arm. "Shoot the moon, now."

She pressed 'Max Bet' and hit the spin button.

Everything on the machine lit up, and she saw that she had won almost two grand

"Oh my God, you did it!"

He placed a finger to his lips.

After she settled down, he told her he'd be at the Coil Bar, waiting for that drink.

A staff member came to her machine and verified her winnings. She was then escorted to the cashier's office, handed twenty one hundred dollar bills, four twenties, one ten, two singles and a handful of change. She stuffed the cash into her purse and walked to the Coil Bar, where he sat waiting, smiling as she came into view.

Two hours and way too many drinks later, she staggered into the parking lot, clutching his arm and kissing him. After taking a quick look around, he eased her into the front seat of his car.

The woman was so drunk that, when the vampire sank his teeth into her neck, she didn't even move. He drank and drank, savoring every drop, until there wasn't anything left, save for a white corpse that would have to be disposed of quickly.

He opened her wallet, noticing her name on her driver's license, and took out all the money.

Tuesday, November 30th, 2010

The vampire left the parking lot of The Sands and made a left hand turn onto 412 South. After waiting interminably for the light to change, he turned onto Lynn Avenue, crossing a steel bridge, thinking that it was badly in need of stimulus money. A couple of blocks up, he saw a small wooded area and stopped the car.

Looking around, ascertaining that no one was out and about at this late hour, he easily lifted Monica Stang's body from the car. He noticed congealed blood around the tooth marks on her neck and put his lips to the wounds, licking it much like a child might lick a Popsicle stick after finishing the treat.

He draped the body over his shoulder and traipsed through the snow until he found a likely spot to dump her, then covered her with fallen branches and brush before piling snow on top of the makeshift tomb.

The vampire then retraced his steps, covering his footprints by pushing snow over them with an evergreen bough.

When he arrived back at the car, he surveyed his work and was pleased that there was no sign that anyone had gone here since the snow had come. He left the area and drove back to town to get a little sleep before having to act like a human being again.

****

James Stang stopped by the station at around six PM claiming that his sister, Monica, had not been seen by anyone since she took off for The Sands around ten Monday night. Monica was known to have an all-nighter on occasion, but she never failed to call him each afternoon to see how he was doing. Normally, a missing person report would not be filed so soon, but these were no longer normal times.

Wednesday, December 1st, 2010

Brian Miller, watching the news, saw a photograph of the girl he'd seen coming from The Sands on Monday night, after midnight. In the photo, a frame from a security camera at the casino, she was kissing a man who looked a bit like the dude who had given him a ride to Hellertown after his car wouldn't start. He had gotten a decent look at the guy's profile while they were smoking, the glow of the butt lighting up his face somewhat. The newsman said that Monica Stang, thirty-one, had been reported missing, and asked anyone who had any information about her to please call 610-555-7396.

****

After the guy had dropped him off at home on Monday night, he had planned on staying in bed for the night after his shower, but several hours after he fell asleep, he started dreaming about winning a fortune, and he woke up knowing he had to get to the casino.

He walked out to the kitchen and grabbed a beer, downing it in short order and when he tossed the empty into his recycling container he figured he'd take the full container down to the trash area. After throwing on a jacket and stepping into a pair of boots, he headed down the steps and out the door.

When he was outside, he saw a friend who was walking his dog.

"Hi George. How are you tonight?"

"Not too happy, Brian. Henry here needed to go out, so now I'm up and I don't think I'll be able to get back to sleep anytime soon."

Brian smiled, hoping George would be interested in going to the casino. He asked him and George nodded.

"I'll pick you up in fifteen minutes."

As Frank looked for a parking space, Brian spotted a man who might be the one who had helped him out. He tried to get a good look at the guy but, just like when he'd been given a ride home, the guy never gave him a full-face look. The goatee and mustache looked right, so he was pretty sure it was the same man. He was leaving with a woman.

****

Brian hesitated for a moment; his fingers hovered over the telephone keypad. Then he punched in the numbers.

"Bethlehem PD. Detective Lasky speaking."

"Hello, Detective Lasky. My name is Brian Miller, and I have some information about the missing girl. I work at the Wood Street Post Office. My car wouldn't start, on Monday after work so this guy gave me a ride to my home in Hellertown. I didn't get a real good look at him, but he had a goatee and mustache. I saw the guy at The Sands around midnight walking in the parking lot with the girl in the picture. My neighbor and I had just arrived to play for awhile. Neither of us could sleep."

"Are you able to come down here to make a statement and see if you can ID the guy by looking at some mug shots?"

"Yeah, I can probably get there in fifteen or twenty minutes."

"That would be good. I have an appointment in town, but someone will take your statement and have you look through some photos. Thank you for coming forward. We want to get to this guy and find the girl as quickly as possible,"

****

Gloria Knecht strolled into the dimly lit bar and slid into a corner booth. When a waiter, came over, she quickly ordered a Bud Light and a Yuengling. After she lit a cigarette, she glanced around, breathing a little easier when she didn't recognize anyone. The beers arrived, so she took a deep pull from the bottle of Bud, then managed two drags from her cigarette before he sat down across from her.

He lit a cigarette for himself and blew smoke in her face. After draining over half the bottle of Yuengling, he belched and said, "What you got for me, Glo-ri-a?" He sneered as he once again blew acrid smoke in her face.

She slid a small box across the table.

He grabbed it, opened it, and whistled. "Nice little stones, sweetheart. Got any more?"

"No. I really have to watch my ass or I'll get caught, sure as shit. Then who'll help pay for your boy toys?" It was her turn to smile. If anyone ever found out that he was a closet fag, they'd run his ass up a flagpole and let his balls flap in the wind.

"That'll never happen, and you know it. Just keep me in these little beauties. That way, nobody, especially that cute piece you just latched onto, will know either of our secrets. See you in a couple of weeks, kid."

She was still in the same booth when Lasky sat down across from her.

"I hope everything went well, Ms. K."

"It went very well, but I don't know how long I'm going to be able to keep up this charade without someone getting suspicious. Those are beautiful fakes we're feeding him, but we've got nothing until he goes to the top and tries to pawn them off. Shit's gonna hit the fan hard then, my friend." She was only doing this for the money Lasky had begun to pay her, after she'd informed him that one of Bethlehem's finest was on the take.

"Perhaps, but I think we should be able to put a wrap on this by Christmas. Then you'll be able to move on with your life."

****

After looking at mug shots for over an hour, Brian Miller was getting bleary eyed. The lighting in the room left a lot to be desired. He glanced up and saw that several of the fluorescent bulbs were flickering on and off in a way that drove him totally bonkers. He wanted a cigarette and a beer, and the silent call from the casino floor kept rattling inside his brain. God, this looking at page after page of men and woman of all ethnicities was about as much fun as casing the countless hundreds of pieces of mail he processed in a day, most of it junk that people would throw away in a heartbeat.

He shrugged as he flipped another page in the book. *Pays the bills, though...*

A face caught his eye. It wasn't the face of the possible kidnapper, but the face of a guy who had started at the post office on the same day he did. A couple of years ago, the asshole had been suspected of stealing packages, so the Postal Inspection Service set him up good. The dude snatched a package and took it home. When he opened it, red powder from inside the box flew everywhere, and a hidden beeper alerted the mail cops. They were breathing down his neck in short order. He'd thrown away a great-paying job because he couldn't help being a klepto. Now the asshole was on the run for evading capture after a major B & E that had netted his accomplices ten grand, some jewelry, and other nifty things they'd found in the house.

Finally, a detective stepped inside the room and asked Brian if he'd had any luck.

He shook his head. "No, Detective. I've been through every photo book you guys threw at me and I only have a couple of pages left."

"Well, you never know, do you? It's like if you lost something, nine times out of ten, it'll turn up in the last place you look. Maybe you'll get lucky with these last few pages. We really appreciate you coming in and doing this. Too bad you couldn't get a plate number, too."

"Yeah, that would have been good, but when I saw them, they looked like they'd just come from having a good time. I figured they were going to his place, her place, or some motel to finish off the night with a little mattress dancing. I just hope she doesn't turn up dead. That would really suck."

The detective nodded and stood by while Brian scanned the last pages of the final mug book.

"Sorry, Detective, no luck. But if anything else pops into my head about the guy, I'll sure as hell give you guys a ring."

****

Mike and Sara ended their shift, two hours late but finally finished. It had been one of those days that seemed to occur during the Christmas holiday season, with people exhibiting a knack for coming unglued at just the wrong time, usually when a cop was nearby. These people seemed hell-bent on finding a parking spot close to the stores they had their sights on. The pair of cops placed tickets under the wipers of cars parked illegally in handicap parking spots, and cars parked illegally in private driveways. The best one, worthy of the day's 'I Am the Dumbest Driver' award, was the driver who squeezed their car, a Hummer, into an alley so tight that that the driver couldn't open either of the doors. Deciding that he must have exited the vehicle via the tailgate, Mike and Sara laughed their asses off as they wrote that ticket.

"Sara, wanna grab a beer?" Mike asked afterward.

"I'd love to, but I have to take a rain check. I'm meeting Gloria later, so I want to head home and get cleaned up and changed."

He nodded. "Have a great time. I'll see you tomorrow for another day of writing tickets, giving directions and watching the insane shoppers. I can't wait until Christmas is over."

"Yeah. Me, too. With luck, the OT will lessen. It's good money, but if you don't have time to spend it, what good is it?"

"Easy for you to say, Sara. You don't have a mortgage."

"I know, but someday I'd like to have a house. Paying rent sucks, too, because you don't get anything out of it. Sure, my life is easier, but… Well, I'm not gonna bore you and, besides, I have a date. So, Corporal McGinnis, if you have no further objections, I'm out of here."

He gave her a playful smack on her arm, and they parted company in the parking lot.

Thursday, December 2nd, 2010

The chosen one for the day would have to be dispatched earlier than normal because of a late afternoon and evening commitment. Killing during daylight hours was always risky, but sometimes the reward was so wonderful that a daylight indiscretion could be tolerated, especially as the time for the final victim drew nearer.

Looking in the rearview mirror, the vampire made a quick inspection. Everything was perfect, as usual. If anyone really got a good look, a whole new persona would have to be put in place. That mailman had come damn close to seeing much too much, and that couldn't be allowed to happen again. There was too much at stake to risk getting caught now.

The South Side was teeming with pedestrians and vehicle traffic. With just over three weeks until Christmas, it seemed that everyone had had the same idea at the same time. As pedestrians passed by, they smiled or nodded their heads; the holiday season seemed to bring out the best in most people, and they wanted to share their joy. The vampire always smiled back. He even spoke to some of the passersby, especially the ones who might fit the bill as the next sacrifice, although he knew that trying to lure one of them to an area devoid of people would be a challenge.

One particular woman caught the vampire's eye, but she was on the other side of the street. He hurried to follow, dodging traffic as he tried not to lose sight of her.

****

Brian Miller was just pulling his key from the apartment mailbox when he heard a car horn toot and the screeching of brakes. He quickly looked toward the street and just caught a glimpse of the man who had taken him home on Monday night, the one who'd been with the missing woman at The Sands, later that same night. He wanted to catch up with him and get a better look at his face, especially the eyes behind the glasses. In the daylight, something about him looked odd, but Brian couldn't quite put a finger on it…

He took a step toward the door, but two of the apartment dwellers, a smelly man and his equally disgusting lady, blocked his way.

"Mailman, I sure hope you brought us lots of checks." They both laughed, and the odor of alcohol escaped from their mouths and assailed Brian's nostrils.

"Yeah, you each got two government checks and the big one from Publisher's Clearing House. Give me a break. How the hell can you people get checks when you don't do shit, all day long?"

Taken aback by the tongue lashing, the man said, "I better not find your ass in this part of town at night, or you could wind up dead, motherfucker." They shoved past him and ran up the stairs, laughing like hyenas.

Brian flipped them the bird, but they didn't see it. By the time he stepped outside, the man was gone.

****

A little over a block away, Mike McGinnis stood outside a storefront, knee bent, the sole of his shoe propped against the wall behind him. He was drinking a cup of coffee and smoking a cigarette while his wife was inside the store, saving him money.

She shopped a lot, but always for bargains. After she arrived home from one trip with her girlfriends, she'd thrown a bunch of shopping bags, with different store logos on them, onto the sofa and smiled. "Well, Mike, I really shopped today."

"So, how much money did you save?" he inquired, hitting the mute button on the TV remote.

"Over three hundred dollars honey."

Mike had just shaken his head and turned the sound back on. He sure as hell didn't need to know how much she spent. She had a good job as a nurse at St. Luke's Hospital. As long as there was enough to pay all the bills and put some away for retirement, he wasn't going to bitch. He got to play all the golf he wanted, and had time to hang out with his friends, so there was no reason to get crazy. Besides, she really looked good in the clothes and jewelry she bought.

He heard a car horn and brakes screech, a little ways up the street, but since there was no sound of metal crunching, there was no need to stroll up there to check it out.

****

The vampire saw the mailman just in time, and he was able to hurry away before Miller could get a better look at him. That asshole was going to have to be dealt with, sooner rather than later, but the woman was his first priority. Quick looks into a few stores yielded nothing but then he spotted her, sitting at a window seat in Molly's Irish Grille. The vampire smiled and stepped inside.

To anyone passing by the window, ten minutes later, the couple would have looked as if they'd known each other all their lives, as they enjoyed their beers and a nice meal, along with animated conversation.

He had brazenly settled across from her, immediately apologizing "I'm so sorry for just sitting down like this, but I am pretty sure you dropped this after you crossed the street." He held out a beautiful silver bracelet with a broken clasp.

"No, I'm sorry, I didn't drop anything."

The man lowered his head, once again apologizing.

"What's the matter, mister?"

"I was so sure this was yours, and now I am totally embarrassed for being so forward."

"There's no need to apologize. Anybody could have made that mistake."

"Thanks, but what do you think I should do with it? It looks expensive." He held it up again.

She reached for it and looked it over carefully. "This is definitely handmade. Sterling silver. I imagine it cost someone a pretty penny." She handed it back. "I guess you could run an ad in the paper and see if anyone responds."

"Yeah, I guess I could, but I'll be leaving town in a few days and..." He handed it to her again. "Would you do it for me, if you wouldn't mind? I'd be happy to pick up your check, for helping me out."

Finally she smiled. "There's no need for that, but if you insist, I hope you will at least have lunch with me."

The vampire flashed a killer smile and, when the waitress came to the table, he ordered. He knew he'd be able to get enough drinks into her to make his task easier.

Less than an hour later, they walked outside, arm in arm. The vampire was given directions to her house and, although killing someone in their own home was not ideal, it had to be done. He'd just have to be careful about disposing of the body.

Oblivious to one another, Brian Miller and the vampire were less than fifteen feet apart. The mail truck Brian was driving passed by the entrance to Molly's as he looked for a place to park. He was starving, and some Irish food would really taste good on this cold day.

****

Once the woman, Emily Burke, realized she was with a monster, she began to cry and shake. As a scream built in her diaphragm and surged upward toward her vocal cords, the fangs drove deep into her neck, and all sound was suppressed.

The vampire drank and drank, not letting go of her even as she started falling backward on the bed. Emily's heart beat faster because there was less blood for it to pump. Clinging to those last few moments of life, she managed to dig her nails into the vampire's cheek. With the last of her strength, she opened the skin there, causing a long, nasty gash. Enraged, the vampire stopped the life-ending process just for a moment to look into the woman's eyes and then, with a sadistic smile, continued taking the last pint or so of precious blood.

After the vampire finished her off, he began the clean-up process. It was growing dark outside, and the time on the clock on the nightstand showed 5:00.

He calmly strolled into the bathroom and looked in the mirror. The gash was already healing and no scarring was apparent. He looked for traces of blood, but found none. He wrapped the body in the sheets and laid the gruesome package on the floor. The vampire found where Emily kept her sheets and promptly remade the bed.

The woman was an extreme neat freak, so he went over things with a fine-tooth comb, but there were no visible signs of a struggle and the room now looked perfect.

No one was outside, so it was easy to load the body into the trunk of the car. After completing that task, the vampire drove off toward the mountain.

A few moments later, inside Emily's home, the phone rang four times and the answering machine kicked in.

"Hi, Em. It's your brother. I've been trying to reach you on and off all day but I guess you're busy. I just wanted to let you know that I was able to catch a flight and I arrive at LVI at 7:30 PM. Hope you can pick me up, but if not, I'll grab a cab and come on over. We have a lot to talk about. See you later, sis."

****

Near the top of the mountain, with the lights of Bethlehem brightening the sky over the city, the vampire parked the car and was just about to open the trunk when a car passed slowly by. The car nearly stopped, the occupants probably taking a look at the vista of the Bethlehem lights, as many people did. Even if they had looked his way, they would only have seen a car parked off the side of the road and a man also looking at the sights.

When the car drove off and was completely out of sight, the vampire opened the trunk and removed the grisly package. After tossing the body over the stone wall, he watched it tumble down the hill and come to rest some forty feet down.

****

Less than one hundred yards away, a poacher named Manny Subits scanned the road through the night scope attached to his rifle. As he swung the scope to the left, he spotted a man opening the trunk of a car and hauling out some sort of large bundle. He watched in surprise as the man dumped the bundle over the edge of the cliff.

What the hell's going on?

Manny had been on the other side of the law for most of his adult life. If the guy was tossing a body, it was none of his business…but he focused in on the license plate of the car. If he had some information about something, maybe somebody would be willing to pay him hush money. A friend of his was a wizard with a computer. For a few bucks, he could probably key in the plate number and come up with some intel that Manny could use as a bargaining chip.

Something rustled the bushes behind him, and the man he was staring at suddenly turned his head in the direction of that same sound. At that, Manny smiled, knowing he really had something now, since he was pretty sure he would remember the face that had just been revealed through his scope. He would put his artistic skills to good use, making a pencil drawing of the person he had just seen.

He waited in patient silence as, not seeing anything; the man hopped back into his car and drove off into the night, none the wiser.

****

Brian Miller was perplexed. All day long, he had searched his memory, but the man had his head turned again, and all Brian could recall was the neatly trimmed goatee and hair, Once again he'd failed to see the man's face, except to note that the man was wearing sunglasses. It was almost as if he knew he'd been seen and was doing everything in his power to retain anonymity. Brian was sure that, if he had seen his face clearly, he would recognize him. Letter carriers were expected to be good with names, but Brian hardly ever forgot a face. It was a talent he wished sometimes he could do without. It was always great when he recognized someone and could also put a name to the person, especially if the person could not make a quick mental recognition of him. Brian liked to be one up because when he was a kid, he hadn't had a silver-spoon kind of life, but he had come a long way over the years.

****

The Brew Works was packed. The work day had ended several hours ago, and the shops were closing their doors. The regulars who had purchased their mugs in advance were bellying up to the bar, engaging in conversation and ordering enough food and drinks to feed a Third World nation.

Gloria was always amazed at the appetites of these college kids, businessmen, shoppers and barflies. It was good for her, though, because the tips far outweighed her salary.

She was in the middle of taking an order when Sara snuck up behind her and blew in her ear.

Gloria turned around and smiled. "Hey, Sar! Can you hang out for a while? I'll be able to take a break in half an hour or so. We have to feed and water the flock, but things should slow down a little, soon. And they called a couple of staff members. They should be here shortly."

"No sweat. I'll grab a seat. Mike's gonna stop by, too, and I think he's gonna bring the ball and chain. They were eating dinner at Mama Nina's but when I called him, he said they were almost finished and they'd stop by for a drink."

"Cool. Try to grab a booth. If not, belly up to the bar and I'll see if I can dig up a table for you in a few." She flew back to the bar with a huge order, the dollar signs behind her eyes lighting up like a slot machine at the casino.

Mike came in fifteen minutes later, visibly shaken. Sitting down hard, he pulled a flask from his jacket and, without saying a word, unscrewed the cap and took a healthy pull. Then he set the flask on the table.

Sara had known him long enough to not say anything. He would talk when he was ready. But she did place her hand on top of his.

"My neighbor, Helen, is dead."

Sara had met Helen a couple of times and had really fallen in love with the gruff, funny German woman. "How did she die?"

He squeezed her hands. "Last night, she was crossing a street in Northampton. Some drunken bastard was driving too fast and ran her down. I hope she didn't suffer. I heard the news from a friend who called me while Jean and I were having dinner. Jean took the car and went home, really upset. But she wanted me to come here and tell you"

Gloria brought two beers and a cup of coffee to the table and sat down. When she saw their faces, she said, "What's wrong, guys?"

Sara filled her in.

"Oh, guys, I am so sorry. What a horrible way to die.

Mike put a hand on top of hers. "Thanks, Gloria." He suddenly smiled in spite of his distress. "God, that woman was so funny, and she and I loved to talk about the Dallas Cowboys. I bet she was wearing that new sweatshirt that she picked up in Atlantic City a couple of weeks ago, the Cowboy star on the front and the words 'Win, Lose or Tie, I'm a Dallas Cowboys Fan Till I Die,'"

They conversed for ten more minutes and then Gloria had to go back to work. Mike and Sara finished their beers, with a healthy dose from Mike's flask poured into the beers, and then they parted company.

"I need to go home and look in on Helen's son, to see how he's doing," he explained, and was relieved to find a cab waiting outside

Friday, December 3rd, 2010

When the alarm rang at six o'clock, Hyram Lasky reached over to shut it off. He wiped sleep from his eyes and rolled out of bed. The aroma of brewing coffee was drifting past his nostrils, but he needed to take a shower first. He had set the timer on the coffeemaker to save some time.

A five minute shower refreshed him and before dressing, he headed toward the kitchen au natural because now he needed a good hot cup of coffee. After he poured a cup and took a couple of deep swallows, he poured some more and took the cup back to the bathroom to sip while he shaved and got dressed. Before he left the house, he woke up his wife and when he backed the car out of the garage, saw that it had snowed again overnight. He shook his head, gauging the amount to be nearly five inches. It hadn't snowed before he went to bed, so it must have really come down in the last six or seven hours. Flakes were still falling, but it seemed the worst of it was over. Mother Nature had caught the weatherman off guard again, since the forecast had given no indication of any appreciable snow.

After he arrived at the office, he checked his phone messages as he quickly looked over some of the notes and letters on his desk. There was nothing new on the Blackman murder or the kidnapping, although he was still hoping that the mailman, Brian Miller, would remember more about the possible kidnapper.

He dug into several reports he needed to look over and figured he'd stay deskbound for the better part of the morning, unless something happened on the street that required his presence.

****

Brian Miller was warm as toast inside the post office, sorting his ass off. Three sets of circulars needed to go out for the weekend, so that meant at least six hundred and seventy five additional pieces of mail each day, to get them to his four hundred and fifty customers. It was frustrating, since they were just bullshit flyers about sales that weren't really sales at all, since the prices were jacked up to accommodate the twenty and thirty percent off deals being offered for the weekend. He knew many more circulars would be on their way between now and about the twentieth of the month. Letter mail to case was relatively light, but the carriers were told that the delivery point sequenced mail, which was machine-sorted in delivery order, would be extremely heavy since two sets of letter-sized advertisements were going to be run through the machines. He had three tubs of first- and second-class flats to case in, and two tubs of delayed mail that also had to be cased in. "Damn," he muttered loudly for others to hear. "Looks like we're going to be at it for over ten hours today. Working in the dark really sucks."

A cute, blonde PTF carrier working in the case next to his yelled out, "Amen, brother." She laughed and stuck her head around the corner. "Man, I couldn't believe it when I looked out my front window this morning and saw all that snow again. We could be in for a really rough winter, as this rate."

Brian turned from his work and saw her smile. His mind was shifting gears, like that of all the other male carriers when they talked to her. She was awesome, and he hoped that she'd be working next to him for the rest of the week. He really enjoyed sneaking a peek at her boobs, since they were always stretching her T-shirt, and when she bent over to lift a tub or tray of mail from the floor, her ass just blew him away.

"Yeah, the Weather Channel sure blew this one to hell and back, didn't it?"

A moment later, their asshole supervisor came into view. "Okay, you two, face your cases and throw mail. We don't pay you to gab on the work floor. Do that on your own time."

They both threw him the finger as he walked past, feverishly writing on his clipboard. Over the past few years, working at the post office had really become a drag. Each carrier had a scanner and had to scan a barcode on the wall when they hit the street. Then, during the course of the day, they all had to scan their first delivery point, going to and coming back from lunch, and their last stop of the day, plus a couple more in between. PR time had gone right out the window, the way they were micromanaged, and service was definitely suffering.

After Brian pulled down his route, he took a quick glance at the blonde's ass before heading out to the street. She really was fine but, he concluded ruefully, way too young.

****

Mike and Sara took a seat, along with all the other cops on the day shift. As they all drank coffee or soda, they chatted amongst themselves, waiting for the shift supervisor to come in and give them a briefing on the events of the past evening and what was expected of them for the day ahead.

He walked in the room and stood behind a lectern as the prattle of voices died down to nothing. "Good morning, everyone. Guess this won't be too good of a day for any of you guys, mounted or foot patrols. We received another gift from God last night – five inches to be exact."

The cops laughed, and some of them pointed stretched middle fingers toward heaven.

The shift supervisor beamed. It was always good to start out the briefing with a little joke, or something else that would persuade the men and women in front of him to give him their undivided attention. He knew that most of the words he'd spew out in the next five or ten minutes would fall on deaf ears, but some of the police officers really hung on everything he said.

"Not a whole lot happened last night except for a few burglaries, some vandalism and a few fender benders throughout the city. There is no news about the identity of the person or persons who kidnapped Monica Stang. Security at The Sands gave us a photo of her, but the man sitting next to her managed to keep his face hidden. Before you leave, you can all pick up a copy to keep with you on patrol. Show it around to see if we can get any more information about her activities from that night. McGinnis and Jameison will canvass her neighbors to see if any of them know anything that will aid in the investigation. Any questions?" He waited a full minute for hands to rise, but none did. "Okay then, hit the street and be safe out there. Oh, I forgot – McGinnis's neighbor was struck by a car and killed, the other night. My deepest sympathies go out to you, Mike."

Co-workers who hadn't known offered condolences as they left for their assignments for the day.

****

The vampire prepared for the new day, reflecting that the five new inches of snow had truly come at a perfect time. It would take that much longer for the body inside the white sheets to be found.

****

Shop owners all around the city prepared to open their doors. Snow almost always meant a bad day for sales but, with Christmas only twenty-two days away, there was room to hope that traffic would be heavier than a Friday any other time of the year. Many of the stores had banded together to have a circular delivered by mail, one that should have gone out yesterday. The brochure listed the names, locations, phone numbers and websites of all the stores that were offering huge discounts for the remainder of the Christmas shopping season. Quite a few of the businesses needed a good December or their doors might have to be closed before the end of 2011.

****

Manny Subits finished his pencil sketch of the man he'd seen on the mountain. He wasn't sure if the guy had tossed a body over the cliff but, if so, the drawing might help lead to his capture. Not that he really wanted to work with the cops, but maybe his assistance would be rewarded with a get-out-of-jail free card from the Bethlehem PD. He looked over his work and decided that the facial features had come out quite nicely, especially the two long teeth he had spotted when the guy opened his mouth. Manny had shaken his head as he drew them, pretty sure he was staring at the vampire that was terrorizing Bethlehem.

He Googled 'Bethlehem Police Department,' found the number he was looking for, and carefully punched in the numbers on his iPhone.

"Bethlehem Police Department. Detective Lasky. How may I help you?"

"Hello, Detective. I have something I think might interest you."

Manny told his story, leaving out the fact that he was a poacher. When he finished, Lasky asked, "Where exactly did you see this happen?"

"On Mountain Road by the overlook area. If you like, I'll meet you there with the sketch and show you where I saw him toss the bundle over the stone wall."

"Yes, I'm definitely interested," he said, as the information he had keyed in on his computer sprang to life, presenting him with all of Manny Subits's particulars. The guy had never been arrested, but Lasky had a feeling that this guy had some baggage he wouldn't or couldn't share. He actually believed the guy, especially the part about the fangs. Maybe they'd be able to identify Jenna Blackman's killer and figure out whether it was the same guy who had kidnapped Emily Burke. "How soon can you meet me there?" Lasky inquired.

"How about eleven? I have a couple things I have to do, but I should be free by then."

"That works for me. What's your cell number?"

Manny went along with the request. He was a little leery about giving that number to a cop but, what the hell; he might be regarded as a hero. And that, in turn, could change his life for the better.

"Okay, I'll see you then. If you're not there, I'll give you a call to see what's holding you up."

"Thanks, Detective. I think you'll be very pleased with my art work."

After they hung up, Lasky called the desk to see if anyone had called in a missing person report. The overworked desk sergeant and clerk assured him that they'd get right on it. After calling several cell phone servers, he contacted T-Mobile to obtain Manny's phone records. When the call records were faxed to him, he jotted down the numbers that Manny had called several times, making a note to check them out later to see if the guy was dirty in any way.

Lasky was still having trouble believing they were really going to hunt a vampire…but what other explanation was there?

****

At ten o'clock that morning, Gloria Knecht arrived at the Brew Works. She had received a call from the manager, informing her that Marie Vincent had called in sick and asking whether she could come in and work a double shift. She had accepted, although she wasn't too happy about it.

"Man, this is probably going to suck, working from opening to closing, but the extra money will come in handy for Christmas," she said the day manager, Vicky Robbins.

"Thanks, Gloria. I called around but the other servers were out or weren't answering their land lines or their cell phones. Don't worry about the long day. I don't think we'll be real busy, with all this snow, but you never know. You'll get a little extra at the end of the day, and you can take that to the bank, honey."

Gloria nodded and started setting up tables, filling salt and pepper shakers and making sure everything looked neat for whoever might stop by. Her cell phone rang and she smiled when she glanced down at the caller ID. "Hi, Sara. What's up?"

"Nothing much, Gloria. Mike and I are patrolling, and I'm bored out of my skull. Mike's taking a pee break so I thought I'd give you a ring. There is absolutely nothing happening out here today."

"Shit, Sara, I'd think that would be a good thing. I'm sure most of the time your job can really suck, riding around in that nice shiny police car, scoping out the vehicle and pedestrian traffic in our fine city. Bethlehem sure as hell isn't like the cop shows on TV, with guns blazing and all that good stuff."

Sara laughed. "True, but it would be nice to have a little action from time to time. We're three hours into our tour and we haven't even written up a traffic ticket. The only thing that made either of us laugh was a real fat-ass we saw come out from a restaurant, slip on the ice, and do a slow roll, winding up on his belly. The gross bastard hauled himself up, dusted himself off, pulled a freaking donut out of his pocket and waddled merrily down the street."

"So what kind of action are you looking for?"

"Honey, I think you know the kind of action I'm ready for."

"Yeah, I do. Unfortunately, I'll probably have to work a double. They called me in to work the day shift and I'll be here until closing, so no fun today."

"That sucks, but I'm sure we can get together real soon. Mike's a little bummed out about it. I think he imagined he'd be getting into my pants one day. Don't think his wife would approve, though."

"Hey, let's face it, Sar. You're pretty damn hot. I'm sure he isn't the only cop who'd like to cuff you to the bedpost."

"Thanks, Gloria. Oops, here he comes. Oh shit, he forgot to lock the barn. The horse may poke its head out." Sara had to take the phone away from her ear because Gloria was really laughing loud. "Guess I better tell him to zip up when he gets in the car. Talk to you later."

"Okay, woman. Take care and be safe out there. You ain't no Kate Beckett, you know."

"Yeah, make sure some irate customer doesn't stick a fork in you. Bye." She flipped the phone closed as Mike slid into the car, and slid him a sidelong look. "Hey, Mike, do you know what's about six inches long and ugly as hell?"

"No, what?" he asked, clearly clueless.

"Your dick. And if you don't zip that thing back into your pants, I'll be staring at the one-eyed snake and calling you all kinds of shitty names." She threw a napkin at him as he looked down and zipped up. "Asshole," she said, and laughed,

****

Promptly at eleven o'clock, a car pulled up behind Lasky's, and Manny stepped out.

He walked over to the detective and shook his hand. Then both of them turned to take a good look at the view of Bethlehem.

"You know, I come here sometimes when I need to figure out a case I'm working on. I find I can analyze better up here than in my office with all of today's technology staring me in the face. Google is great, but the human mind is better than a computer for figuring out the little details. I'm still wondering what you think might be in this for you." Lasky lit a cigarette and looked over at Manny.

"Detective, I'm just doing what any other good citizen would do. I'm sure you've already checked up on me and found that I'm pretty clean."

"Yeah, I did. Any theories on why somebody would be up here in the dark, walking in the woods? Especially someone who doesn't have any ties to anyone in this area?" When Manny didn't reply, Lasky shrugged. "Maybe my detective instincts work overtime too much. So, where is this thing supposed to be?"

Manny walked toward the stone wall at the edge of the overlook and peered down the hill. With all the snow, he had a tough time, but he finally saw a hump about forty feet down. "I'm pretty sure that snow-covered lump is a body, wrapped in a white bed sheet, but it'd probably be a bitch to get down there."

"I got that covered with one phone call. But first let me see the sketch you made."

Manny reached inside his coat and then he saw Lasky reach inside his coat, as well.

Manny sucked in cold air, wondering if Lasky was reaching for his weapon. "I'm only going to pull out the sketch, like you told me to. Don't get crazy, now."

When Lasky relaxed, Manny handed over the sketch.

Lasky looked it over. "How far away were you when you saw this guy?"

He pointed across the street toward the spot. "Up there on the hill, near that tree shaped like a Y."

"Looks like about a hundred yards. Tough to see someone at night from that distance unless you had night binoculars or a night scope on a rifle. I'm not going to ask which one you had. The fucker does have fangs, doesn't he?"

"Yeah. Scared the hell out of me when I saw him."

"Okay, I'm calling for some cops to go down that hill and see what's under that hump. You don't have to stay if you don't want to because my guys probably won't be here until around noon."I am cautioning you not to leave town until my investigation is complete."

"I would like to get back to my life until the lid breaks off this story. I suppose you want to keep my sketch."

"Roger that. If there is a body down there, this sketch is going out on the wire as soon as I get back to the station. The media is going to have a field day for sure but if you want me to keep your name out of the five o'clock follies, I'd be happy to do so. Eventually, though, there's bound to be a leak. Seems like there always is." Lasky still hadn't been able to find out who'd leaked the vampire news after Jenna Blackman's murder. He shivered, picturing her stone-white corpse.

"Nah, I don't think I'll mind getting my fifteen minutes of fame. I only hope someone really cool plays me when the movie comes out about the Christmas City Vampire." Manny turned and strolled back to his car, whistling softly.

****

The three cops Lasky called to the scene were working hard at their task. They tied a long length of rope to the back of the van and then descended down the hill, getting some traction in the fresh snow as they lowered themselves along the rope. Lasky kept a close watch and directed them to the snow-covered hump. Once they arrived at the spot, they were able to let go of the rope and keep their balance by holding on to tree trunks and digging in the soft snow.

The first officer started brushing snow from the top of the hump. In a minute or two, he found the white sheet and started digging around it with his gloved hands. The other two officers helped out, and soon they had the bundle completely uncovered. One of the officers took several photographs before and after uncovering the bundle. Tying the rope around what was definitely a body, they climbed back up to the stone wall and, once they were standing on the other side, started pulling the rope up. As they did this, the sheet became partially dislodged, exposing a bit of an arm that was nearly as white as the snow. Before moving any further, more photographs were taken.

When the body had been lifted over the stone wall and laid on the macadam, the men gently removed the sheet, revealing the body of a woman, her neck bearing fang marks, a silent scream etched on her face. The sheer look of terror frozen in her dead eyes made the men feel a little sick. Lasky grabbed the camera and took a few pictures before recovering the corpse.

After they loaded the body into the back of the van, the two vehicles wound their way back down the mountain, and delivered their grisly find to the police morgue.

****

Brian Miller finally punched out at six thirty PM. His workday had lasted over eleven hours, and he was exhausted. He wasn't the only carrier to return late, and he saw that several trucks were still out on the road. He was tired, but he was also starving, and he needed a drink badly, so he stopped at The Crossroads Hotel and had a cheesesteak, fries, and three glasses of Yuengling. Afterward, he headed home. After a shower, he grabbed another beer from the fridge and settled into his favorite chair to watch some TV.

Helped by the beers, he dozed off, only waking as the Channel 69 news began with a breaking story about a woman's body being found, while the screen displayed a sketch of the probable killer.

Brian sat straight up, staring. It was definitely the guy who'd given him the ride, the one who'd been escorting the missing woman, Monica Stang, to a car in the parking lot of The Sands, early Tuesday morning.

"There is even speculation about the suspect being a vampire, based on the fangs he is displaying in the sketch. The woman, Emily Burke, 32, was reported missing by her brother, late yesterday evening, after he was unable to contact her for several hours. If anyone has seen this man, please call the Bethlehem PD as soon as possible."

Brian jumped up from the chair. The vampire had killed again, last night? He raced to the bathroom and just managed to lean over the commode in time for the beer and cheesesteak to spew from his mouth into the bowl.

Afterwards, shaken, he wiped his mouth and staggered back to the TV, which was offering side stories about the fictional vampires found in books, movies and TV shows.

"So there you have it folks. We could be dealing with a fictional character that isn't fiction anymore. If you see this person, please consider him dangerous and call the police immediately at the number displayed here on the screen."

****

At the Brew Works, conversation had come to a complete stop; patrons and staff alike had their eyes glued to the television screens, iPhones, Blackberries, and iPads. Disbelief was gradually replaced by growing fear, and many of the patrons paid their tabs and headed out the door to their homes. Others were intent on calling friends.

Soon, the bar was nearly empty, with the staff busily cleaning up, wanting to head home but dreading the moment when they would have to step out into the darkness, especially alone.

The manager called the police station, requesting escorts for some of the more frightened customers and employees who refused to leave because they would have to walk home, but the request was denied. Those who had no fear volunteered to escort the frightened people to their vehicles

Gloria Knecht called Sara and asked if she could come to her apartment, so that neither of them would have to be alone.

Saturday, December 4th, 2010

By dawn, the story had broken nationally. Google reported that the number of hits to vampire-related websites was staggering. As the sun began its march to the west, television and internet viewers in every state were greeted with the story of the 'Christmas City Vampire.'

Manny Subits smiled as he watched a webcast. Lasky was using the name he'd coined. He quickly bought the .com domain name 'Christmas City Vampire,' in case anyone had the bright idea to steal his thunder and make money from his idea.

Fear took a firm grip on the people living in the Lehigh Valley, spreading to all points of the compass as the sun climbed in the sky. By ten o'clock, grocery stores were overburdened by shoppers. One shelf after another emptied, with stock people reloading them as quickly as possible. The run was much like that before an impending snowstorm, as people piled bag after bag of both essentials and non-essentials into their cars. By eleven o'clock, there wasn't a loaf of bread or quart of milk to be found. Some of the larger chains had gouged their prices on staples and were making a killing.

Beer, liquor and wine were the next things to go, as the rush on state stores and distributors was in full gear. The panic continued its march, and the same kind of rush began in all fifty states as soon as stores opened their doors for business.

Word spread rapidly via phone calls, text messages and e-mails. Never in the history of the country has such fear and pandemonium set off this type of chain of events. Looting was becoming a problem, and the police in every town and city had their hands full, dealing with theft. Double-parked cars blocked the streets, and 'vampire' was uttered so often that it truly became the word of the day.

Since the stores in downtown Bethlehem were hardly seeing any traffic, many of them closed. The sidewalks were emptying of pedestrian trade. Before long, the shopping district of Bethlehem looked like a ghost town in the Old West, lacking only wind-blown tumbleweeds to complete the effect.

Detective Lasky kept staring at the sketch of the vampire, seeing something but not knowing what it was. The gnawing thought in his mind was that he knew this person, yet the recognition wouldn't click, and it was driving him crazy. The mailman, Brian Miller, had called to tell him that the sketch definitely was the guy he had now seen on three occasions, and he, too, seemed certain that he knew the guy.

Sara was awakened by a phone call from Mike. All police personnel were to report as soon as possible. Gloria was still sleeping, so she kissed her on the forehead and headed out for what she suspected would be a long, long day.

By noon, the only people on the street were emergency personnel and those few civilians who seemed not to care whether they might be attacked by a vampire, due either to depression or to a fanatic belief that, if they were bitten, they would then live forever and become all-powerful. In the meantime, neither Jenna Blackman nor Emily Burke rose from the dead, rendering that theory seriously suspect.

Monica Stang's remained undiscovered.

The vampire watched the news and scanned websites, knowing that capture was now possible. That would make the hunt for the next victim a huge challenge. But two more victims were needed or the mission was doomed to failure.

****

Lasky could not take his eyes from the sketch. He tried to look beyond the features of the man, and it was becoming more and more frustrating. He got up from his desk and took a short walk to the bathroom, relieved himself, and then he headed back to his office. As he passed an administrative assistant in the hallway, they greeted one another with a nod. After walking a few more steps, a thought struck him so forcibly that he had to stop, lean against a wall and catch his breath. "Damn," he muttered out loud, and raced back to his office and picked up the phone.

"This is Lasky. Is there a police artist available?" He listened to the voice on the other end. "Thanks!" he said, then lifted the receiver again and dialed another number.

After four rings, someone answered. "Donmoyer Graphic Design. Eleanor Freed speaking."

"Hi, Ellie. It's Hy Lasky. How are you doing?"

"I'm fine, but you must be going crazy with all this vampire news. I can hardly believe it."

"Yeah, I know. This could be the most earthshaking news story since the birth of Jesus Christ. I need a favor."

She listened intently as he explained, and finally said, "Yeah, I think I can do that. I'll go to the website and pull the picture, then fool around with it and give you several different versions. As soon as I'm finished, I'll e-mail them to you. You have an interesting concept there, Hy. I'm looking at the sketch right now, and I see where you could be right. Besides, I wasn't doing much anyway. The two appointments scheduled for today fell through, so I need something to keep me busy."

"Oh, Ellie, you are such a bullshitter. You always find something to do when you're at work. Tell you what, when you're finished printing them out, give me a call and I'll meet you at the Brew Works for a couple of drinks."

"Sounds good. This shouldn't take too long at all. I bet I'll have the work done in less than an hour. I am sooo good at what I do." She laughed, but it was true. She was a magician on her PC, and she had every tool available.

"Okay, Ellie, I'll look forward to your call."

****

Mike and Sara were cruising the streets but there wasn't a whole lot to see. Many of the stores were closed because of the panic, and very few people were venturing out on foot. A bar on Broad Street was doing a brisk business, however, and Sara figured that, no matter what was going on, short of nuclear war, drinkers would continue to sit in bars, drowning their troubles and talking about everything under the sun.

She took out her cell phone and hit speed dial.

After five rings she was directed to voice mail. "Hi, honey, it's me. I just wanted to see how you were doing. You seemed pretty scared last night and I gotta admit, I was, too. Give me a call when you get this message. Love you."

Mike glanced her way. "You fell pretty hard and fast, didn't you?"

She looked at him and saw that he wasn't being sarcastic. "Yeah, I did, Mike. Gay relationships are more difficult than heterosexual ones. I think gay people tend to be more..." She searched for the right words "...more volatile than straights" She paused again, swallowing hard, unable to formulate precisely what it was that she wanted to say.

"Have you always been gay, Sara?" He touched her knee, and she knew he wasn't trying to be an asshole.

She thought about some of the military people she knew and sometimes drank with. People always seemed to be asking them whether they had ever killed anyone. She remembered something one of her vet friends said one night after a few beers and a random guy came to their table after seeing his veteran ball cap and thanking him for his service, then he asked that question. 'You know, that is not the best question to ask a combat vet, because some of us would just as soon slap you silly than answer. Most people on this planet hold life very sacred, but there are things you have to do in war to live, and to keep living is a strong motivational force to take the other guy out before he takes you out. There is nothing personal in killing the enemy, but talking about it, except to other vets who had the same experience, is something we generally tend not to do.' Her friend looked at the man with eyes cold and hard as steel and a smile that would make you melt. The guy simply nodded, said, 'I'm so sorry,' and walked away.

The military parallel was not the same, but she knew that she could trust Mike with her life, so answering his question wasn't so difficult, after all. "No, Mike. I think I was like any other teenage girl. All we did was talk about boys and tell each other our fantasies. Sometimes we lied to each other like hell, wondering which of us were truly virgins and which had their cherries popped by some guy who said the right words and did the right things.

"I was seventeen when I fell in love with a nineteen-year-old guy. We dated for about a month and one night, the mood was right and I was ready. His folks were out for the evening, so after a couple of glasses of wine, a nice, warm fire roaring in the fireplace, I felt I was ready to experience sex for the first time." She looked out the window at the empty street.

"Anyway, we went up to his room. The petting grew heavier and heavier, and I made the first move by taking off his shirt. It didn't take long before we were both naked." She looked toward Mike. "Am I making you uncomfortable?"

He shook his head.

"Well, once we were both naked, he climbed on top of me, and it was painful when he entered me. I cried a little, so he stopped and just held me for a few moments. I kissed him hard and he continued. When he finished, he didn't hop off, he just kept holding me and kissing me, but I felt nothing. When he got off of me and went to the bathroom, I quickly dressed and left the house, crying like a baby. "

"He must have been stunned to see you gone."

She shrugged. "He didn't call me for a couple of days. Maybe he was afraid he'd hurt me, or that I needed some time to sort out my first sexual encounter. When he finally called, we talked for a little while and when I told him I was pretty sure I was a lesbian, he freaked and cursed me up and down."

"Did you ever see him again?"

"Yeah, a couple of girlfriends and I were hanging out at the mall when he and some of his friends approached. He looked at me and smiled wickedly. 'Guys, this is Sara, the lesbo I fucked the shit out of last week. Guess she couldn't handle a ten-inch dick and she's reverting to eating pussy for the rest of her life.' He laughed at me and gave me the finger. One of his friends didn't laugh, so I figured he was a closet homo. My friends, who were all straight, taunted me and walked away, laughing.

"It was tough at school, and we still had a couple of months till graduation. Things sure have changed for the better in the past thirteen years."

She had been looking at Mike the whole time she was talking, trying to see what kind of reaction he was having, but he listened intently, glancing her way from time to time.

When he turned toward her once again, shock registered on his face like a gaudy neon sign. "You're thirty years old. I would have never believed that."

They talked enthusiastically about subjects they both knew something about, even football. Mike was surprised by her knowledge but gave her a good razzing when she told him she was a New York Giants fan.

"Hey, listen, I can get hold of some tickets for the next Cowboys and Giants game. Do you think Gloria would like to go?"

"Yeah, Mike, I think she would. I'll ask her, as soon as she calls me back."

****

Lasky was sitting at a table in the Brew Works when Ellie sat down across from him. "I worked on a couple of variations of the sketch." She handed him a folder.

As he looked them over, she saw the blood drain from his face. He passed the one electronic drawing back to her. "Do you recognize this person?"

"Nope. Is it someone you know?"

"Yeah, it is. I'm sorry, Ellie, but I have to get back to the station and round up some men. Thanks to you, I think we may end this reign of terror today. I owe you one, big time."

"You don't owe me a thing, my friend. I was glad to help out."

****

An hour later, after their wide-ranging conversation had finally died down, the radio sprang to life.

"This is Unit Two," Sara responded. "Go."

"Meet Detective Lasky at 227 West Broad Street. No lights or sirens, and park at least a block away. Do you copy?"

"Affirmative, Base," she said. "No lights and sirens, and park at least a block away." She put the mic back in the cradle and began to cry. "That's Gloria's apartment building. I hope she's okay. Mike, I'm scared."

"Hey, it could be something else. Don't go ballistic on me. We're cops and we have a job to do."

They arrived and walked to the front of the building. A SWAT team was there, clad in bullet-proof vests and helmets with shields. All of them were carrying M-16s and one had a battering ram.

As Sara approached Detective Lasky, she saw the look on his face and she knew something must have happened to Gloria.

He handed her the sketch.

As soon as she looked at it, she knew what it meant: Gloria Knecht was the vampire.

She fainted.

Sara regained consciousness quickly, but it took several more minutes before she was steady enough to stand up. Even though she had loved Gloria she knew what she had to do. "Okay, I'm ready now. How are we going to get her?"

"I sent four men to the rear of the apartment in case she tries to bail. I want to take her alive so she can be questioned about what she is and whether there are any more like her, but if we have to kill her, we will. I don't want any of us dead today." Lasky grimaced. "Hopefully we'll surprise her and take her alive, but we've never dealt with anything like this before."

"If it comes to killing her, I want to be the one to put a bullet in her brain or her heart. We gotta do whatever it takes."

"Okay, Sara, when they bust down the door and go inside, you get in there right behind them. Actually, when she sees you, it might slow her reaction time down just enough that we can take her alive."

After silently climbing the stairs, two SWAT officers battered the door down and stepped inside. Sara immediately followed. They stormed through the rest of the apartment, but Gloria Knecht was nowhere to be found. The coffee pot was still perking and the toaster was still warm.

"Shit, how the hell did she know?" Lasky demanded, then got on his hand-held radio and spread the word that she was gone.

The search continued for the rest of the day, but the vampire had vanished.

By the time the evening news aired on TV, Gloria Knecht's picture had been distributed to the media nationwide, and the number of self-professed vampire hunters grew from a few to thousands. Facebook set up a page, and over twenty-five thousand hits were recorded.

By the time that midnight rolled around, the number of 'fans' on that page had swelled to millions. There was probably not a soul in the country that was unfamiliar with what had become the most recognizable face on the planet.

****

Several hours earlier, Gloria Knecht had taken refuge in an abandoned building at the former Bethlehem Steel complex. Along with some clothing hurriedly stuffed into a suitcase, she brought her makeup case and several male and female wigs. She also had foam padding to alter her shape as she began to work at changing her identity again.

Gradually, the persona of a slightly overweight fifty-something woman took shape. Dressed in an oversized Lehigh University sweatshirt, a long, black, matronly dress, some gaudy beads, white socks and sneakers, a gray wig and granny glasses, she was confident that she could pass as one of the many middle-aged women, a little down on their luck, who frequented The Sands.

Pure luck had led to her spotting the police cars pulling up a block from her apartment building. She had bailed out the window and climbed up onto the roof, keeping low until she was able to climb down to street level.

Since then, her picture had been spread all over the World Wide Web, which was actually working in her favor. People seemed to feel safer about going out, now that they thought they could put a face on the danger, and it was hard for the police to stop anyone who wanted to get out and have some fun and a few drinks. When Gloria arrived on the casino floor, she was amazed to see the number of people playing the slots and table games. She strolled around for a while, with no one paying her any particular attention. Eventually, she found a seat at a quarter machine next to a shapely thirtyish woman who was dressed to the nines. Gloria peeked at the machine she was playing and saw that the woman had several hundred dollars' worth of credits.

Sitting down, she said in a husky voice, "My! You're doing quite well tonight. I hope I'll be as lucky as you are."

The woman looked at her with disdain, simply nodded her thanks.

Soon, however, the woman was losing steadily, while Gloria worked the machine she was playing, winning several hundred dollars. She noticed the woman glancing her way from time to time and, when she caught her looking again, she tapped the machine twice and spun the reels. When she was rewarded immediately with another hundred and twelve dollars, she laughed out loud. "It works every time," she said, looking at the woman again.

"You have a way to beat these machines by tapping them?"

"Well, it's a little more complex than that, my dear, but it really isn't hard to learn. May I show you?"

"Absolutely. I'd love to win some money before I have to leave." She looked at her watch. "I've got about an hour."

"That'll be plenty of time. I need to slow down a little anyway. If I win more than twelve hundred, the taxman will get some of it, and we don't want that, now do we?" She cackled at her own humor. She hit the collect button and stuffed the voucher in her purse, then inserted a fifty-dollar bill.

Ma'am...?"

"Maggie, Maggie Sommers."

"Hi Maggie, I'm Alicia Wingate. Nice to meet you."

"You too, Alicia. I do so much love to teach people how to beat these machines. I've been doing it for over half my life and I have a pretty nice nest egg, spread out at different banks, you know."

"No, why?" Alicia inquired.

"I don't like to keep all my eggs in one basket."

"Whatever, Maggie. So what do I have to do?"

Gloria paved her way with different size bets, winning some and giving some back. After a few bets she said, "Okay, Alicia, now play a max bet and after you spin the reels, tap the front of the machine twice.

Alicia shrugged her shoulders but did what she was told…and won a jackpot of nearly seven hundred dollars. "That was so cool, Maggie! Can we do it again?"

Forty-five minutes later, Alicia cashed out for over two thousand dollars, and Gloria pocketed fourteen hundred and seventy two dollars.

"Alicia, I'd like to ask you for a favor."

"Sure, what can I do for you?"

"My son dropped me off on his way to work. Could you give me a ride to Fourth and Hayes Street?"

"Of course. I'd be glad to help you out, after the good luck you brought me, but you have to promise to meet me here again tomorrow night at seven o'clock."

"Sure. I'd love to play with you again, Alicia. This has been so much fun."

****

The police found the body of Alicia Wingate seated behind the wheel of her car, some six hours later. Her white corpse was drained of blood and two tooth marks were visible on her neck. And the panic began all over again.

Sunday, December 5th, 2010

Lasky had awakened much too early, but he couldn't fall back to sleep. He got up, prepared his morning coffee and, as it was perking, stepped outside to see if the paper had arrived. It wasn't in front of his door, so he looked both ways and saw the carrier approaching. He waited while the man walked up the pavement and handed him The Morning Call.

"Mornin'," the man said. "All this terrible news about a vampire loose in our city. How are you guys going to catch her?"

Lasky took the paper. "I don't know. I mean, the crap you see in books and movies says you can kill a vampire by driving a stake through her heart, but a local author published a book several years ago, and his theory was that you couldn't use a stake to kill a vampire. He figured that a vampire could only be killed by fire, by drowning, or by severing its head from its body. I think he may have been on the right track, but we're going to try everything humanly possible to destroy her. If we ever find her."

"Yeah, well, good luck with that. Bethlehem is a big enough city for somebody to lay low, so your work may be cut out for you."

Lasky nodded. "You could be right. You be careful out there. I don't want to lose you. You've been a great carrier, all these years."

"Don't worry about me. From what I've been reading and the news I've been watching on TV, it seems like she's only after women, and young women at that."

Lasky nodded again. "Well, be careful anyway. You have my number if you see anything."

"Yup. I put it in my cell phone. See you soon."

"You, too. Have a great day."

When he walked back inside the house, the phone was ringing. He ran to answer it, figuring that if someone was calling him that early, it wasn't going to be good news.

"Lasky."

"Detective, I'm afraid I have some more bad news. We found a dead woman named Alicia Wingate. Her body appears completely drained of blood. Her purse was still in the car, but there was no money, only her IDs and credit cards."

"Okay, get over to The Sands, and have security pull up the tapes from last night to see if Alicia had been playing, and if Gloria Knecht was nearby. If she has a Sands card in her purse, take that with you."

"Will do. Oh, by the way, there is a news truck here and they filmed us checking out the vehicle. We kept them as far away from the scene as possible, but I'm sure this is going to be on the news very soon now."

When he finally hung up the phone, he was deeply frustrated. Gloria was involved in an ongoing investigation he was heading up, and now that was shot to hell. He had never had any kind of a clue that she was anything but a human being trying to do right for him.

Lasky turned on the news. The vampire shit was still the lead story on every network.

Moments later, the video shot from the scene flashed onto the screen, and he knew it wouldn't be long before the news was sent worldwide on the web.

****

By the time most church services began, millions of people had heard the news. It was good for church attendance; their pews were overflowing and so were the collection plates. The panic had shifted into high gear again.

Promptly at ten-fifteen, the contemporary-service music leader welcomed everyone. Then the band kicked into high gear with a rocking Christian song. People rose to their feet, singing and clapping their hands to the driving beat of the drums, guitars, and organ. They sang their hearts out and clapped wildly; their fervor to get in touch with God was the strongest emotion many of these part-time church goers had experienced in a good long while. The congregation had swelled to double its regular number of worshippers.

Mike McGinnis, his wife, Jean, and Sara Jameison were lucky enough to be among the final congregation members to find a seat in the gym, where contemporary services were always held. The traditional service, held in the sanctuary, was also packed. Every available seat was taken, and people lined not only the sides but also the center aisle. The number of participants at those two services alone numbered well over a thousand people.

After the first song ended, everyone sat down. One of the pastors stood in front of the band and offered his greetings. "Thank you all for coming out today under these circumstances. I know many of you are frightened, but God will see us all through this crisis and order will be restored, not only in Bethlehem, but throughout the country. I know that Christians around the world will be praying that this vile creature, a demon in human form, will be destroyed."

Mike, Jean and Sara clung to every word spoken and every song sung during that one hour and fifteen minute service, especially Sara, who was still in a state of shock from knowing she had fallen in love with a murderer.

****

When Lasky had driven to within a half mile of The Sands, he saw news trucks from all the local stations parked in every available roadside spot. He heard over the radio that the major networks were coming in, as well. He slapped the wheel; until Gloria was captured or killed, Bethlehem was going to be the focus of every freaking news service in the country. They'd get people and cameras here as quickly as possible, every reporter wanting to be the one to record the final chapter of this incredible story.

Monday, December 6th, 2010

At one minute before six, Ken Glass said, "Morning America begins right now."

As usual, the show opened with a video clip. Generally the program was geared toward politics, but today it was all about vampires. The clip showed Detective Lasky's statement to the media from the previous night: "Our investigation revealed that Alicia Wingate, whose body was discovered a few hours ago, was seen on the security tapes of The Sands Casino. She was seated next to a grey-haired woman dressed in a long, black skirt, a brown Lehigh University sweatshirt, sneakers and white socks. The woman wore granny-type glasses and was a little on the heavy side, but we surmise, since footage shows the two women leaving together, that she is the vampire, Gloria Knecht, in disguise. When she murdered Jenna Blackman, she was disguised as a man with a mustache and goatee, so we are asking all citizens to be extremely vigilant. Do not talk to anyone you don't know, and do not accept or offer rides to strangers. I cannot stress enough how dangerous this woman is."

The well-known face came on camera. "Good morning, and welcome to Morning America. I am Jackie Ciamacco, and I am here with Joe Fida, Ken Glass, and Tom Trainer, live from in front of the library in beautiful Bethlehem, Pennsylvania. Joining us today are Detective Hyram Lasky from the Bethlehem Police Force, Jim Blackman, husband of Jenna Blackman, who was the vampire's first victim, Sally Rogers of the Bethlehem Brew Works where Gloria Knecht was employed, and Vincent Malone, manager of The Sands Casino. Lady and gentleman, welcome to Morning America."

During the first hour, all of the guests were interviewed. When they broke for yet another endless commercial, Joe was called to the side of the outdoor set.

Back on the air after the commercials, the camera locked on Joe Fida. "I've just been informed that we have a Skype feed with a woman, Melissa Lambert, of Steubenville, Ohio. "Miss Lambert, good morning."

"Good morning. It's a pleasure to finally get an opportunity to speak with you. I have been a fan for many years."

The camera zoomed in on Joe and Jackie, smiling and offering their thanks.

"Melissa, Joe told me before you came up on Skype that you are certain you know the vampire, Gloria Knecht."

"Well, Jackie, I did know her, thirteen years ago. But her name then was Jane Harmon."

"So, what can you tell us about her, Melissa?"

"When I saw all the news on TV, I decided to do a little digging. You see, Jane disappeared ten years ago, around Christmas, and I never saw or heard from her again... until this vampire news came out. Like I said, I did a little digging, and I found out that five women from our area were reported killed or missing between Thanksgiving and Christmas, that year. Of course, I had read about it, back then, but it really never crossed my mind again until things started happening to women in Bethlehem. I would make a guess that Jane is going to kill again. And here's the really interesting part -- the final murder occurred on Christmas Eve. That afternoon was the last time I saw Jane, at least until I saw your sketches and pictures of Gloria Knecht on TV."

The Morning America cast and their guests were stunned. "This happened exactly ten years ago, Melissa? Are you sure about that?"

"Yes, Jackie, I am absolutely certain, and I'm sure you'll have your geeks working on the information I've given you and coming up with the same timeframe. I'm just wondering how long she's been killing five women a year every ten years, and why?"

"That is a great question, Melissa. Thanks for chatting with us. Taking into consideration everything you said, I'm urging all law enforcement agencies to look back over their records as far back as possible to see what murders and disappearances may have occurred in their towns and cities from 1990 on back."

"You're welcome, Joe, and I sure hope someone kills that bitch before she takes any more lives."

The camera panned back to Jackie. "If anyone has information about similar incidents, please call 610-555-2379. We're going to stay in Bethlehem until the vampire is captured or killed, or until

Christmas arrives, hoping that it will put an end to this decennial rampage."

****

In Lansing, Michigan, Carl Anderson, a paraplegic and super-hacker, was busy at his keyboard, utilizing all the search engines at his disposal to dig into the past, determined to see what he could come up with on similar incidents that had occurred in years ending in zero. He wheeled his chair a little closer to the desk and leaned into his work. When he lost his legs seven years ago in an industrial accident, he had been devastated and wanted only to die. He had always been an active outdoorsman, and sitting in a wheelchair for the rest of his life held no appeal at all.

A few weeks after beginning his therapy, he began to read books about computers. He learned how to read code, and soon thereafter he hacked into a public works site in California. He discovered that the department head was skimming several hundred dollars a week from special projects, and sent an anonymous tip to the town mayor. A few weeks later, the man was caught dipping his fingers into the cookie jar again and was fired on the spot. He was arrested, charged with grand theft larceny and was sentenced to five to ten years. His finances were gone over with a fine-tooth comb, and seventeen men and women wound up in prison for their participation in the shady dealings.

The newspapers broke the story and, even though Carl couldn't take credit, he was finally able to make sense of his disability and move on. He created a spiderwebnet which gave him more reach into computer systems all around the country, and it wasn't long before he found another company, this time in Maine that was being bilked for hundreds of thousands of dollars a year. Once again, his anonymous tip led to multiple arrests.

If he wanted to continue with his covert business as the Internet vigilante, he knew that he'd have to increase his income. He offered to build websites at an extremely low price, until he became very well-known for his creativity. Over the past five years, he had begun making some serious money, and was able to furnish his office with the best computer equipment on the planet.

In just a few hours, he found references to a similar set of occurrences in the time frame of November 26th to December 24 in Sayer, Kansas. He immediately sent an email to their police department, urging them to check the inactive files and newspaper archives for the information that the Morning America team requested.

Personnel were assigned the potentially monumental task, but it turned out not to take long for them to uncover material on murders and disappearances that occurred during those dates in 1970, at which point the officer in charge immediately called the number from Carl's e-mail. People who had given their names and statements in the files were contacted to see whether any of them had any recollection about the slayings. Fortunately, one person, Barbara Johnson, was found and interviewed. She agreed to tell her story to Joe and Jackie via satellite on Tuesday's program.

Police departments across the country were digging as deep as they could to see whether they could come up with something more.

Before Christmas a large number of people would claim their fifteen minutes of fame.

Tuesday, December 7th, 2010

December 7th – "a day that will live in infamy," as President Franklin D. Roosevelt said during his speech in 1941 after the Japanese attacked Pearl Harbor – seemed destined to become historic for an entirely new reason.

By six AM, when Morning America came on the air, they had information of murders and disappearances for the years 1950 and 1970.

****

Online entrepreneurs struck gold by selling wooden stakes and crosses, all with the tips sharpened, ranging from raw pine to deluxe vampire-killing kits of polished mahogany. Prices varied from as little as ten dollars to as much as a thousand. Home Depot and Lowes climbed onto the bandwagon, as well, selling stakes and crosses as quickly as they could stock them.

Garlic growers and sellers also shifted into high gear, offering intricately woven wreaths to be hung on doors and windows, along with garlic sachets for out-of-home protection and even garlic spray, much like pepper spray, to disable potential vampire attacks.

T-shirt manufacturers were quick to respond to vampire mania, producing shirts with logos like I Love Vampires, the word love inside a heart, Vampires Suck, and Fangs for Everything.

Bookshops all over the country sold out of their entire stock of vampire-related books and magazines, and placed huge orders for more. TV shows and DVDs with vampire themes sold equally briskly. Money was rolling in, providing the economy with a much-needed jolt.

America had gone insane, not least since no one even knew whether stakes or garlic would do the job. The country as a whole was betting that horror writers had been right in their claims about how to kill a vampire or, at the very least, protect yourself from having one get close enough to harm you.

****

Back in Bethlehem, Jackie Ciamacco was interviewing the stars of Vampire Journals, who were treating the subject with respect, although Joey Esposito, one of the shows vampires, was asked to get into character and answer questions the way he would respond.

When asked, "What would it really take to kill a vampire?' he responded, "Well, it would be easy to kill my brother," looking toward Steve Tourve. "The man doesn't take care of himself because he refuses human blood, plus he is so google-eyed for Jenny that it would be real easy to sneak up behind him and stake him before he could even run a comb through his hair."

Elena Van Dyke, who played the character of Jenny Listak, totally lost it and laughed so hard she had to catch her breath.

When the laughter, which became contagious, died down, Esposito turned quite serious. "I'm glad I could help you viewers relieve a little bit of stress, but this is truly not a laughing matter. I would never in a million years have believed in the existence of vampires, and I am as shocked as all of you are. Please do not interact with strangers, or accept rides from them, especially you kids who think you're indestructible. Dealing with something we know absolutely nothing about is difficult at best, so don't try to be a hero. I fervently hope that someone out there can shed some more light on this woman, Gloria Knecht. Maybe there's something we're all missing that could help the police capture or kill this creature."

After he finished, the cardinal rule of communication was broken; there was none for nearly a minute. Dead air was totally frowned upon in the TV and radio business.

Jackie broke the prolonged silence. "We'd like to thank all of our guests today. I couldn't agree more with what Joey pointed out. Please do not put yourself in any danger by associating with someone you don't know. It's been established that Gloria Knecht can disguise herself as both men and women. Look around. She could be standing next to you right now. See you all tomorrow, live from Bethlehem."

When the cameras stopped rolling, the stars spent time with the people in the library courtyard who had come to watch the show. Surprisingly, there was no stampede to shake hands or talk to the celebrities. Instead, questions were asked of all the personalities, although many could not be answered.

Afterward, the five TV stars hopped into a waiting limo and were taken back to the Hotel Bethlehem. From there, they all went to the Brew Works for a few drinks and some bar food, and once again were treated like regular human beings, although there was more than one guy taking good long looks at Jackie's and Elena's legs.

****

Officer Colleen Mathias of the San Diego Police Department spent most of the day combing through the files of the deaths of five women during the critical time period in nineteen eighty. She discovered something that might or might not have any connection to the other decenniums. She dialed the emergency number given by the Bethlehem Police Department

At the end of her conversation with the detective, he asked for her number and said he'd get back to her. He had to check with the coroner's office to see if that information had been noted in the autopsies. She knew it would probably take a long time to get any information returned to her, but she also knew this was something that should probably be kept from the public. Turning back to her regular office work, she looked forward to quitting time and a trip to the beach for an evening weenie roast and a lot of beer. Although she believed that Gloria Knecht was the only vampire in existence, Coleen was still troubled. If Gloria wasn't killed in this ten-year cycle, Coleen would only be thirty-seven in a decade, when the next killing cycle began, which would still put her in the approximate age group of all the victims known so far.

****

Near midnight, Gloria Knecht disguised as a thirty-something man, booked a room for two weeks at the Comfort Inn on Highland

Drive in Bethlehem. It was a nice place and would suit her needs very well.

She needed two more victims, but there was still plenty of time to accomplish those missions. She wanted to be as comfortable as possible while she planned her attacks.

She had to laugh at the comments Jackie Ciamacco had made, telling the audience, "Look around. She could be standing next to you, right now." The guy she was standing next to had absolutely no clue who she was when he looked at her, smiled, and then looked away again. Her disguise worked perfectly, and she figured she might go back to the library, either before or after she killed again.

Gloria took a long, luxurious bath and then crawled into bed under the covers. The coldness was always the worst thing about being a vampire, but soon that would be gone forever. She was so longing to become human again.

Wednesday, December 8th, 2010

There wasn't a room to be found within thirty miles of Bethlehem. The city was beginning to overflow with its regular seasonal tourists. Even more were drawn to the city to do a bit of Christmas shopping. Some were there hoping to witness or hear about the vampire being slain, as something they could tell their families and friends about. Human curiosity was a strong emotion. More people were taking multiple day trips to The Sands. Hundreds of people in nearly as many cars were tying up traffic, just to see the place that the vampire was calling home. The majority of them didn't seem seriously concerned about the possibility of being killed, and some of them had heard that Maryann McGee, star of the American News Network Evening News, was coming to the city to do live reports for the remainder of the Christmas season.

Cops were working hard to maintain some kind of control, as people were parking their vehicles anywhere they pleased. Many visitors and residents were seen sporting web belts around their waists, filled with varying sizes of wooden stakes. It was getting totally out of hand, and arrests for disorderly conduct were taking up far too much of the officers' time: arresting the offenders, taking them to the station for booking, filling out all the forms, and then either locking them up or sending them to the city courthouse to pay their fines in front of judges and magistrates, who were also burning both ends of the candle.

Lasky and the other detectives frantically followed up on the flood of leads being called in. Most of the calls were nonsense but they had to consider that there might be one that led to the vampire's location. The entire police force was exhausted and wanted this over as quickly as possible.

Lasky was briefed about the call from Officer Mathias, but no information arrived from the coroner. They were busy, as well, because of an influx of deaths, many from heart attacks and suicide. Deaths were also being chalked up to raw fear. Routine paperwork and phone calls were pushed to the back burner.

With all of the people arriving in town, there was a boom in sales for nearly everything that was made in Bethlehem or bore a Bethlehem logo. Most stores that sold plastic or ceramic Stars of Bethlehem were sold out of them before the end of the day.

Rock and Roll junkies shopped for anything related to John Lennon, since it was the thirtieth anniversary of his murder. Aside from the Christmas music being played everywhere, the only other music heard in stores or restaurants was Lennon's or the Beatles' music, on the theory that giving the people what they wanted would open their wallets even wider.

Restaurants and diners were having a great day, with patrons having to wait up to an hour for a table, booth or a stool at a counter. At the current rate, food would probably run out before too long.

Gloria Knecht, wearing a hooded sweatshirt and sunglasses, stood at the corner of Main and Broad Streets, surveying the human and vehicle traffic. She rubbed her hands together, pleased that it would now be much easier to find a victim. Townies weren't going to interact with strangers, but the temporary immigrants didn't know Jack from Jill and were talking to everyone. She had struck up several conversations in the hour she'd spent walking the same two-block stretch. Nobody had a clue that they were taking to a vampire.

She asked a man if he had the time. He smiled at her, looked at his watch and said, "It's one thirty-five." She thanked him and smiled. Ken Glass of Morning America smiled back, having no idea that he had just spoken to the most wanted person on the face of the earth.

As she continued her walk down a street packed with shoppers, she saw something that made her smile. Fifteen feet away stood a woman who looked a lot like her, and she couldn't resist having some fun. She screamed, "Oh my God, it's the vampire!" She pointed at the woman, who was also looking around, and Gloria saw fear etch her face as the thought that she might be the next victim.

The first person to tackle her was a strong-looking teenager. When he leaped and grabbed her around the thighs, the woman went down in a heap. It didn't take too long before she was being pummeled by passersby of all ages and both sexes.

Moments later, the vampire, hidden in an alcove beside the Wired Café, watched the cops approach.

****

Mike McGinnis and Sara Jameison pushed people out of the way, yelling for the crowd to stop what they were doing. It took several minutes before they were able to restore order and cuff the last two people who had been beating up the hapless woman.

"What the hell are you doing?" Mike screamed at the two prisoners.

Sara knelt on the street and looked the woman over, trying to see the extent of her injuries. Her left eye had been gouged out of its socket and was hanging on by a thread. After seeing the mess on her face, Sara feared that the woman was dealing with internal injuries, not just a couple of broken bones and multiple contusions. She felt for a pulse and found one, although it was weak. She heard one of the prisoners tell Mike that someone had yelled out that this woman was the vampire, and that he had only been trying to assist in her capture when all hell broke loose.

As she called for an ambulance, Sara stood up; scanning the gathering crowd of rubberneckers for anyone was laughing or seeming to enjoy this situation that might cost an innocent woman her life. She glimpsed a figure in a hooded sweatshirt standing deep within an alcove between two buildings, but a man in the crowd stepped forward, trying to take a picture of the fallen woman with his cell phone, and Sara had to step between him and the injured woman and demand that he put it away before others would begin to crowd her. By the time she looked again, the alcove was empty.

Moments later, the siren became louder as an ambulance turned from Broad Street onto Main Street. Two paramedics clambered out and hurried to the victim. As they took the woman's vitals, one of them looked up at Sara, his expression warning her that the woman had very little chance of surviving the beating. She was loaded into the ambulance, which then sped away toward St. Luke's Hospital.

Mike, Sara and the two other cops began the slow process of interviewing the witnesses. Over the course of the next ten minutes, they talked to a number of people and ascertained that someone in a hooded sweatshirt had yelled out that the beaten woman was the vampire. Pandemonium had erupted as people feared for their lives.

Sara looked back uneasily toward the alcove again. When she closed her eyes to try to mentally focus on the person's face, she realized it could have been Gloria, and she began to cry.

Fifteen minutes later, they received the word that the woman had died before she arrived at the hospital. Her name was Ellen Markley and she lived in Reading. The paramedics figured she had come to town to do some shopping. Her family was being contacted.

***

A few blocks up, on Broad Street, Gloria Knecht calmly drank a cup of coffee, waiting for news coverage of the beating to appear on TV.

Thursday, December 9th, 2010

Sara Jameison reported to work, still deeply shaken by the conviction that she had actually spotted Gloria Knecht standing in that alcove and hadn't recognized her in the moment. Granted, Mrs. Markley would still have died, but....

Mike came over to her. "How are you doing, Sara?"

"I'm still shook up. If only I'd recognized Gloria standing in that alcove, we might have had a chance to end this crazy reign of terror."

He put his arms around her and gave her a big hug. "Don't be so hard on yourself, kiddo. It could have happened to anyone. There was a lot going down yesterday. Besides, you didn't get a good look at her face. Maybe it wasn't even her."

She lifted her head from his shoulder. "It was, Mike. I'm sure."

"Okay, so you're positive it was her. There still might not have been much we could do. I'm really concerned about the way the people in this city are reacting. We have nuts out there carrying stakes around, like people carried guns in the Old West. What's to stop any of them from making a mistake and stabbing an innocent person, thinking it's Gloria in disguise?"

"Yeah, I guess you're right. It's gonna hurt for a while, but we have a job to do, so I guess we better get in there for the briefing."

They had barely taken their seats when Detective Lasky entered the room.

"We have some information but I honestly don't know what it means. Yesterday, a police officer from San Diego called. She'd been going over files from late 1980, and discovered that all the female victims at that time in her city were having their menstrual cycles when they were attacked and killed. If any of you guys and gals have a theory about how that might figure in, let's hear it."

Sara raised her hand. "Maybe the vampire has a terrific sense of smell and could smell the blood, and that was the way she chose her victims." If so, the number of potential victims could be reduced by having this knowledge. "Maybe we should get this information out to the general public so that those women, at least, can better protect themselves by staying at home or not going out alone."

"Good idea. I'll have that information released, this morning. We also know that the Christmas-season murders go back to at least 1960, and that they've all occurred during this late-November to Christmas Eve timeframe. I don't have anything more to add. While you're out there, please be safe. And if you see or hear anything out of the ordinary, act on it immediately. This woman wears a wide range of disguises, so it's going to be really difficult to pin her down. We are checking every phoned-in lead, no matter how insignificant or off-the-wall it may seem. Most of them are bogus, but we can't afford not to check them out. Have a good day."

All the cops assigned to that tour were leaving the building, with none of the normal amount of chatter and jokes being told. They were cops, ready to tackle the situation head-on.

****

Brian Miller was excited. He'd heard that Maryann McGee was in town, and he really hoped to get a chance to meet her. Maybe her people would even contact him, since he'd had a couple of face-to-face moments with the vampire.

As he made his rounds, he was totally vigilant, wondering if he would see Gloria Knecht again, and whether, if she was in one of her disguises, he would recognize her.

The day flew by. When he returned to the Post Office at three-thirty, he found a note on his case, directing him to call the producer of The Evening News with Maryann McGee. Elated, he phoned from the workroom floor, while he was still on the clock. It was a no-no, but he really didn't give a rat's ass if a supervisor gave him a rasher of shit over it. He was going to meet Maryann, and that might well turn out to be the coolest thing that ever happened to him.

After copying down all the information, he raced home, took a shower, shaved and put on his best suit for the interview. Then he looked at himself in the mirror, gave a nod of self-approval, and left his home. It would only take twenty minutes to get to the Hotel

Bethlehem, where he'd been told to give the valet his name and his car would be safe.

Once inside the majestic hotel, he was ushered to the 1741 on the Terrace dining room where he and several others involved in the vampire business would have a meet-and-greet with Maryann. Then they would have a round table discussion, which would air in segments over the next three evenings. The room was elegant with floor to ceiling windows offering a great view of a number of shops on Main Street. Beautiful Christmas decorations were masterfully placed and even in the midst of the terror Bethlehem was facing, the holiday spirit could not be diminished.

Brian had a couple of drinks and ate some great finger food, compliments of ANN. One by one, the others arrived. The first person to show up was Detective Lasky, followed a few minutes later by the two police officers, Mike McGinnis and Sara Jameison. Everett Gardner from the coroner's office arrived a few minutes later, and the last one to enter the dining room was Vicky Robbins, the day manager at the Bethlehem Brew Works.

Small talk ensued for several minutes, until Maryann arrived and was introduced to everyone. As soon as she finished greeting each person with a smile, the producer had everyone take their seats in a half circle. Brian watched excitedly as Maryann took her seat, since it showed off her fabulous legs.

The interview was being taped, so he wasn't worried about saying anything stupid; the editing process would save him. He also knew he probably wouldn't have more than a couple of minutes of air time. Still, whatever she asked, he wanted to present himself as an intelligent, articulate guy.

The producer spoke first. "Hi, everyone. We're going to have Maryann ask each of you several questions, and you can take as much time as you need to formulate your answer. Some of the questions will be personal, but the interview is mainly to capture your thoughts about the events that have occurred here in the past two weeks. So everyone relax and take a couple of deep breaths. This won't hurt a bit." He smiled and received the laugher he wanted, designed to help Maryann's guests relax.

"Brian, it's wonderful that you could come here tonight to give us some insight into your several meetings with the vampire, Gloria Knecht." Maryann flashed a smile and Brian damn near wilted.

"Thanks, Maryann. First of all I'd like to say that I've been a fan of yours for a long time."

She smiled and nodded.

He went on to tell her about the day his car broke down, when Gloria Knecht, disguised as a man, gave him a ride home.

"Did you have any idea that you were in the company of a woman, or did her disguise really make you believe that she was a man?"

"I was totally fooled by her appearance. I'd seen and spoke with Gloria on several visits to The Brew Works and, even though she wasn't the most stunning woman I'd ever seen, she is – or should I say she was – a looker. Finding out later that she'd fooled me completely in her disguise as a man really blew me away."

"When did you see her again?"

"Actually, it was later that same evening, Monday the twenty-ninth. I was restless at home and decided to relax at The Sands Casino. When I arrived, about two o'clock on Tuesday morning, I saw her, still disguised as a man, walking with a woman in the parking deck. By the time I found a parking spot, they were gone, but when I heard about the woman's disappearance, I called Detective Lasky and told him what I'd seen."

Maryann turned to her left. "Detective Lasky, how did you find out that Miss Knecht might have been the person who abducted the woman from the casino?"

"We received several calls from the missing woman's brother, but we weren't overly concerned because less than twenty-four hours had passed since he had last heard from her. Once the information was released to the public, Brian called us and told us what he had seen. We reviewed The Sands' security tapes and found images of Miss Stang playing a slot machine next to a man who fit the description of the suspected killer of Jenna Blackman, who was slain on Black Friday, after she closed her shop. Obviously, we all thought we were dealing with a male suspect, at that time."

Maryann turned to Vicky Robbins. "Gloria worked for you for some time as a server. Did you have any idea that she would turn out to be a vicious killer?"

"No, I didn't. She was always a hard worker. Almost every time I called her to come in on her day off, she did it happily. Several times over the past couple of weeks, she took off for a few hours, telling the night manager that her mom was ill and that she had to take care of her. Even if the bar was short staffed, we gave her the time off, and she always came back later in the evening. I guess one of those times was when she gave Brian a ride home."

The conversation continued for another hour, with everyone discussing how they had known Gloria.

Sara sat quietly for most of the interview, until Maryann asked her about the relationship she had with Gloria. Tears filled Sara's eyes as she told the world that she was gay and had fallen in love with Gloria almost immediately. "Maryann, she seemed like such a tender, loving woman that I still find it hard to believe that she's a vampire. I would never have guessed in a million years that she could have been responsible for so many deaths over the past forty or more years." At that, she broke down and was comforted by Mike McGinnis.

Mike looked into the camera and stated, in a hardened voice, "Gloria, know this. We will find and destroy you, you fucking bitch."

"Thank you all for an enlightening interview. If you have time, I'd like to chat with you all over drinks and hors d'oeuvres. I am absolutely famished and, to be perfectly honest and extremely un-Maryann like, I really need a couple of belts. This is some really scary stuff, you guys."

Before the interview was to air, the producer toyed with the idea of letting the profanity stay, but decided in the end that keeping his job was more important than sending that word out over the airwaves.

****

A mile or so away, Gloria Knecht, in the guise of a middle-aged, well-dressed woman, was spending a gloriously relaxing evening at one of Bethlehem's largest events for the Christmas season, Christkindlmarkt. The holiday event lasted from November 26th until Christmas Eve.

As she leisurely strolled through the maze of vendors, crafters and food stands, she felt altogether human. By the time Christkindlmarkt closed its doors for the season, she would have selected her final victim and broken the dreaded curse. Then she could live a normal life until the day she died.

Stopping to admire an antique painting depicting a snow scene, she allowed her thoughts to drift back a century and a half to the fateful day that the curse had befallen her.

****

On Thanksgiving Day, in 1860, Amelia Gibbons paid a visit upon her aunt and uncle in Salem, Massachusetts.

She had travelled nearly twenty miles in a horse-drawn buggy over rough roads, all by herself. Her parents truly did not want her to travel such a great distance alone, but she was twenty-five years old and would not be put off by such concerns over a woman travelling alone. Amelia was always the most adventurous of the five children born to her parents and although it took a great many days of pleading her case, they finally acquiesced, allowing her to make the journey.

Her father had urged her to take his long rifle and a knife, in the event she would possibly run into men who would do her harm She was fearless, but she agreed to carry the weapons to protect herself from would-be thieves She felt that she would be able to handle herself quite well, but she inwardly admitted that the trip could pose some threats.

Amelia loaded the buggy with dried fruits and vegetables and several yards of cloth to give to her aunt as a present. Her aunt was a wonderful seamstress and would enjoy making a new dress for herself.

Her travel was only interrupted once, when a man on horseback rode up beside her buggy. He simply nodded his head and smiled when she looked toward him. He rode beside her for several miles without ever once saying a word, and that did bother her, but she decided that, as long as he didn't cause any trouble, she would not agitate him in any manner.

When they approached an area where both sides of the road were lined with trees, she became a little apprehensive about his intentions, as he seemed to become nervous. Was he going to attempt to violate her by stopping her buggy and carting her off into the trees, where he would not be seen doing what he might do to her?

"Sir, may I ask why you are riding with me?"

He finally spoke. "I don't very much like women travelling alone, and I thought I'd offer you some protection until we get through these trees. I've traveled this way many times, and on several occasions I have run into dangerous men."

"Why did you give me that strange look when I first saw you?"

He cocked his head. "I'm not sure what you mean, miss. I was just smiling at you."

"Your smile frightened me, especially when you didn't speak to me at all."

"I'm so sorry. I don't talk much, and I rarely if ever speak to a woman, unless she speaks to me first. I truly do apologize."

She relaxed a little, but she still wasn't willing to become too friendly, so she simply nodded as they continued through the wooded area.

Once they were in the open again, he said, "Salem is only a few more miles on this road, and I think you'll be safe the rest of the way, so I will ride off now. I have to ride about three miles west to my destination. Thank you for allowing me to guide you through the most dangerous part of your trip." He nudged his horse into a trot and then a full gallop before she even had a chance to answer him.

When she crested a ridge, Salem was less than a mile away, and she was thankful to have arrived unharmed.

Her aunt and uncle heard the buggy approach and came out from their modest house to greet Amelia and help carry the fruits, vegetables and bolt of cloth into their home. After taking everything inside, Amelia's uncle headed into Salem.

A fire was roaring in the fireplace because the day had become colder. Above the flame was a rather large wild turkey roasting. Amelia realized that she was very hungry but she knew dinner would not be ready for several hours. She also caught the scent of a freshly baked pumpkin pie, and dried apples were cooking in a stewpot hanging from the spit that pierced the turkey.

"Everything smells wonderful, Aunt Rebecca."

"Would you like a slice of pie?"

"I would adore a piece, and a cup of coffee, if you have any."

Amelia devoured her pie and two cups of coffee over some small talk, then asked Rebecca if it would be alright to go exploring the town for a little while.

Rebecca told her that would be quite alright, but to be careful because she had heard that a witch was in town.

"A witch? I thought all the witches were long dead."

"Yes, there are very few around anymore, but yesterday one of the children in the village was frightened nearly to death by the sight of her."

"I'll be careful, Aunt Rebecca, but you know that I always have to have an adventure or I am not pleased."

"Yes, I know. So scoot and have a good time. Try to be back before dark, for that is when the dinner will be ready to eat. While you are gone, I'm going to start measuring the beautiful bolt of cloth you brought for me. Your uncle is probably having a few pints with his friends, so make certain he comes back on time, too."

"I will." She turned on her heels and raced out the door, ready to explore Salem.

Many of the residents were busily preparing their Thanksgiving dinners, so there weren't many people she could have a talk with. She looked in storefront windows to see what kind of merchandise was inside, and took the time to play with several children kicking a ball about.

The time passed quickly. As she looked down a side street, she saw that a woman had fallen, and raced to her aid.

"Are you alright, ma'am?" She helped the woman back to her feet.

"Yes, I am. Who are you? I've never seen you around here before."

"I'm Amelia Gibbons. I'm here today visiting my aunt and uncle for Thanksgiving."

"That's lovely, my dear. I wish I had a family to visit on Thanksgiving but I have been alone since my husband passed, two years ago on this very day."

"How terrible. You must be very lonely."

"I am. Would you do me the honor of coming to my home for some tea?"

"It is getting late and I promised I'd be home before dark, but a cup of tea would certainly taste good."

"Wonderful. Please walk with me."

They strolled along for a few minutes before arriving at the woman's house. Once inside, the woman bolted the door behind her and cackled. 'I've been waiting for someone like you for a very long time."

Suddenly frightened, Amelia tried to get past the woman, open the door and run to her aunt and uncle.

The woman blocked her way and pushed her to the floor. "I need you to stay here, Amelia, so that I can give you a gift."

"What kind of a gift would you give to a perfect stranger?"

"Why, the gift of eternal life. Wouldn't you like that?"

Amelia was able to kick the woman to the floor and scramble to her feet. A moment before she would have thrown the bar from the door and escaped, the woman dragged Amelia to the floor again and knocked her unconscious.

When she awakened, her hands and feet were bound with rope. Lifting her head, she saw that she was lying on the floor within a large circle drawn on the wood with flour.

"What are you going to do to me, you witch?"

The woman smiled.

"I am indeed a witch, but my curse will be broken once I transfer the curse to you by taking some of your blood and offering it to the master. The ritual will take several hours, but once I am finished, I will no longer be a witch. However, you, my dear, will become a vampire. Your curse can only be broken by killing five women between now and the day before the celebration of the birth of Christ. You must do this every ten years until one hundred and fifty years have passed. On that last Christmas Eve, when you sacrifice the final woman, you will once again become human and live out the rest of your life."

****

Gloria's reverie was interrupted when a woman tapped her on the shoulder and asked where she had bought the necklace she was wearing.

Gloria smiled at the woman. "I bought it at Sephora, in the Lehigh Valley Mall."

"Well, it's beautiful. Have a great Christmas."

"You do the same."

Gloria followed at a discreet distance as the woman walked on through the tent, stopping frequently to browse at the merchandise displays. She also saw something several times that bolstered her decision about where the final victim would be slain.

"Unfortunately," she murmured under her breath, "you won't be around to see another Christmas."

Friday, December 10th, 2010

After a video showing the crowd of people that had gathered at the previous day's beating of the woman on Main Street had run its course, Jackie Ciamacco came on camera. "Good morning, everyone, and welcome to Morning America, live from the library in Bethlehem, Pennsylvania. The video you just saw was shot yesterday. Ellen Markley, thirty-one, from Reading, Pennsylvania, was brutally attacked and killed by a blood-thirsty mob. Two people were arrested, but a number of people participated in what was a fatal case of mistaken identity. According to reports, an unknown person yelled out that Mrs. Markley was the vampire. She was immediately tackled, then pummeled for several minutes before police arrived to stop the horrific beating. She died en route to the hospital, leaving behind a husband and two young children. Our prayers go out to them."

Joe Fida came on camera. "We at Morning America are all saddened by what occurred here yesterday, and quite frankly, we are frightened that something like this could happen again at any time. The population of Bethlehem has swelled by many thousands of daily visitors. Some have come here to shop, while others only seem to be here to say they were in Bethlehem when the vampire was captured or killed. I have always been amazed by the mentality of people who feel the need to gawk at human suffering. You see it every time you are held up in traffic – people who slow down or even stop to stare at an accident. Many people go to auto races hoping to see a spectacular crash, and, I just don't know, Jackie."

"Yes, Joe, you are absolutely right, but no matter how often the public is urged by the police to stay out of the city, it seems that twice as many as the day before come here anyway." She picked up her iPhone and read a text message. "I'm sorry to say that there was another killing last night, near the Christkindlmarkt tent. The bloodless body of a woman, Joyce Carrington, thirty-five, who resided in Macungie, Pennsylvania, was found less than an hour ago in a dumpster. The police are actively investigating this crime. They are requesting that anyone who was there last evening and may have seen anything unusual should call the emergency number running on the crawl at the bottom of your screen."

****

An hour before Morning America came on the air, Detectives Hyram Lasky and Miles Steele arrived at the scene where Joyce Carrington's body was found. Escorted to the dumpster, they took a good look at the stone-white corpse of a once-beautiful woman. Her neck had been ripped open, and there was a slight tinge of blood on the edges of a wound the size of a tennis ball. Even after having witnessed many mutilated bodies over his long career, Lasky found himself turning away from the sight.

His eyes were red from lack of sleep, and the only thing that seemed to keep him going were large daily amounts of coffee and cigarettes. He was starting up a terrific cold from being so worn down, but he couldn't afford to take any time off until Gloria Knecht was disposed of.

"Who found the body?" He asked one of the cops on the scene.

A young maintenance worker was brought to Lasky. He appeared in a state of shock and Lasky understood completely. The man probably had never witnessed anything as gruesome before in his life.

"You okay, son?"

The man nodded but he was shaking, so Lasky put his arms around the man and tried to comfort him as best as he could. When the man settled down, Lasky released his hold. "I'm Detective Lasky. Can you tell me what you were doing before you found the body?"

"Yes, sir. I work for the city. I was here cleaning up the mess that people leave every day when they come to Christkindlmarkt. I had a trash bag full of garbage, and I took it over to that dumpster." He pointed to the one where the body had been found. "When I opened the lid, there she was, dead as hell. I tossed my cookies and then called the cops. I've never seen anything like that in my life, and I never want to see anything like it again. My girlfriend is scared shitless. She left the city yesterday to go stay with relatives in Sarasota, Florida. Detective, please find this vampire soon. I miss my girl."

"We're doing everything in our power to find Gloria Knecht, but it's not going to be easy. I have no idea what kind of disguise she was wearing last night, but the victims seem to have no hesitation about going with her, and they wind up dead. You can go back to work now, and thanks for calling it in."

The young man nodded but his eyes were pleading for Lasky to end this nightmare without delay.

****

Watching Morning America, Brian Miller had heard the news about the latest slaying. He was so upset that he thought about calling in sick to work, but the Post Office was shorthanded, and the overtime money always came in handy as a way to feed his gambling fever.

He wanted a piece of Gloria Knecht real bad, and he hoped that somehow he would be one of the men and women who helped to kill her.

After spending nearly two hours in the office, casing mail and watching a stupid video that all employees were forced to watch from time to time, he pulled down his route, placed all the trays, tubs and parcels in a big orange hamper, and took the load out to his truck.

The weather was a little cold, but the sun was shining brightly. He actually began to whistle a Christmas song as he filled the back of his mail truck. As he prepared to take the hamper back into the office, an elderly man, supporting his weight on a cane, limped into the parking lot and called out, "Excuse me, could you please help me?"

Brian walked over to the man to help ease his obvious pain as he walked. "Morning, sir. What can I do for you?"

"My car stalled, up the street." He pointed to a white Toyota Camry parked partially on the curb. "You're the first person I've seen. I hoped you might have a cell phone I could use to call Triple A."

Brian handed him the phone and waited while the man placed the call. After he finished, he handed the phone back to Brian. "Thank you so very much. They say they'll be here in less than a half hour."

"You're very welcome, sir. Have a great day."

As he turned and walked back to the Post Office, Gloria Knecht smiled inwardly. She now had the mailman's cell phone number.

****

Earlier, on Morning America, Jackie came back on camera. "Since this vampire business has begun, I've done some research on the subject. I found thousands of websites that deal with this material, and I was enlightened by the information on many of those sites. Since all vampire books are fiction, I had our research team check to see if there were any local authors who have had a book or books published on the subject, and I was particularly taken by one book, <u>The Final Vampire</u>, published by Delancy-Hartman Press in 2004. The author, Roy Clayton of Hellertown, is with us today."

The camera cut to Roy Clayton. "Thank you Jackie. I never thought I'd someday be talking about a fictional character that is now real."

"In your book, you are adamant that a vampire can't be killed with a wooden stake to the heart, going against everything that has ever been written about vampires. Why do you feel that way?"

"In my research, I've read that because a vampire is in effect a magical creature, the only way to destroy one is by killing it with something that was once alive, ergo wood. As time has progressed, since the first written words about vampires, we have seen them defying the rules that were first offered about their existence." He turned his head, coughing slightly and then taking a sip of water. "Excuse me. Vampires have gone from being impaled in their coffin, leaving behind a skeleton to the vampires of today who turn to dust when a stake pierces their heart. I just wanted to take the legend a step farther and make it a little more difficult to slay one."

"So how do you think this real vampire can be destroyed?"

"I think it can only be accomplished in the three ways I described in my book. The creature has to be beheaded or burned. I also thought that a vampire could be destroyed by drowning, but they don't breathe to begin with."

"Interesting theories. I certainly hope that we'll all be able to find out what can finally end Gloria Knecht's existence, and sooner rather than later."

Saturday, December 11th, 2010

Christmas was only two weeks away.

Although the mood of the people walking around the shopping districts was somber, there was still enough holiday spirit to keep them focused on their missions.

Most of the stores had been able to restock, after the initial rush on Bethlehem-related items, and the bookstores had ordered, or were in the process of ordering, every vampire-themed book they could get their hands on. Online, Amazon and Barnes and Noble were seeing increased sales in that type of book, as well.

Also, since Roy Clayton's appearance yesterday on Morning America, sales of swords had begun to skyrocket. Individuals determined to claim a piece of Gloria Knecht, most notably her head, were laying out outrageous sums of money for the tools they thought they would need if confronted by a vampire.

One entrepreneur from Morristown, New Jersey, experimented with loading bullet tips and balls for flintlocks with minute slivers of wood. His firing tests worked and so, as soon as he was certain the guns would not blow up in the users' faces, he began to market them online. An experienced bow hunter, he also developed a wooden tip for arrows. It took him a while to determine the correct size to keep the arrow on a true flight, but when he did, that product also went on his website.

Police officers countrywide were alarmed by the number of people carrying guns and wooden stakes, knowing that it probably wouldn't be long before these same folk would also be carrying swords in sheaths on their belts. And although many of these people had watched the Morning America interview, it appeared that they weren't willing to put all of their faith in the one vampire writer who differed from all the others. Wooden stakes were still selling briskly.

****

Carl Anderson informed the police about his hacking activities, stating that he was willing to serve the time but he wanted to be placed under house arrest until he could determine how far back Gloria Knecht's reign of terror stretched. All of his research led him to believe that she had been committing her heinous acts since at least 1900, but he needed time to dig deeper. He asked to be allowed access to the archives of police departments and newspapers nationwide, hoping to discover more about this woman who seemed to be impossible to capture or kill. Some references were found that the female victims had indeed been having their menstrual cycle when they were brutally murdered, but he still didn't understand why this was so.

The World Wide Web was buzzing, alerting women who were in their cycles or would be before the end of the year to be extremely cautious and to stay in their homes as much as possible. They were also urged not to walk the streets alone.

****

Brian Miller walked into the paralegal's office at the law firm of McGuire and Schmidt and threw the mail onto her desk. "Hi ya, sweetheart. How ya doing today?"

Jessie Sterling smiled at him and leaned back in her chair as he poured two cups of coffee. "I'm great, Brian. Not enjoying having to work on a Saturday, but you must be in seventh heaven after schmoozing with Maryann McGee, last night. I can't wait to see how you look on TV."

Brian handed her a steaming cup of coffee, with two sugars and a touch of French vanilla creamer swirling in the black liquid. Then, laughing, he dropped his mail satchel onto the floor and sat down. "Yeah, it was pretty neat. She is really a nice lady."

"Lady, huh! I imagine you took more than a couple of long, hungry looks at those famous legs of hers. Was she was wearing a short skirt." Jessie batted her eyes a couple of times for effect.

Brian made a cutting motion with his free hand to the middle of his thigh. "Sucked up that view as much as I could, Jess. She sure does have honeys there."

"Bet that wasn't the only thing you wanted to suck," she said, and roared at her own little joke.

He offered a wink. "No, it wasn't. Man, you see a woman like that on TV and wonder what she really looks like in person… I certainly wasn't disappointed."

He took a big swallow of coffee before adding, "Her boobs are pretty nice, too."

"How does she compare to Jackie?"

"Jackie's sweet, but I wasn't really close enough to make out all her features. I watch Morning America before heading out to the job almost every day, I'd say and I'd say she's a close tie in the leg department with Ms. McGee."

"This vampire business is some serious shit, Bri. It's got me afraid to step outside alone. It really is a pain in the ass when my car is parked a couple of blocks away, because that woman could be out there lurking, posing as Lord knows what. It seems like she can disappear in plain sight, and I don't know if the cops or the freaking vampire hunters I've been seeing all over town will get to her before she kills again."

"Yeah, I think that's going to be a tough go. I only wish I could get my hooks into her. Imagine the person that does bring her down. They're going to be on the gravy train for a long time. There'll probably be a book and a movie about this whole deal. I wouldn't mind being in on that one, kiddo."

She offered a look of dead seriousness. "I wouldn't want to see you mix it up with her. You'd wind up dead." Turning a little silly again, she started riffling through the mail, throwing piece after piece into the trash can. "Who the hell would bring me all this junk if you were gone?"

"Hey, there'd be a long line trying to land my route, although in the past couple of years more good people have moved out and been replaced by lowlifes. I wish I were older so that I could get the hell out, even if I had to work part-time. Working five out of six Saturdays has never appealed to me, but I gotta admit that in spring, summer and fall, getting that weekday off to play golf is not too bad. The weather is really starting to play hell with my joints. When I get home from work, most of the time all I want to do is crash."

"Well, I'm glad you're not an old fart yet."

"Yeah, but I'm really jealous of one of my neighbors. He carried mail for twenty-one years, after working nearly fourteen at

Mack Trucks. He retired a couple of years ago and now he works three days a week for a courier service. That man has it made.

"Actually, he was on Morning America earlier. He wrote a couple of books, one about a vampire, and his theory is that you can only take one down by beheading or burning the bitch. Guess I'll stroll down to his house later to see if he has any copies on hand. If his books start selling like hotcakes, he'll be able to give up his part-time job sooner rather than later."

"Talking about later, Brian, I'd like to ask you a favor, if you don't really have anything going."

"Sure. What do you need?"

"Well, I have to take some papers to a client at the Hotel Bethlehem. If you'll come, I might even spring for dinner and a couple of beers. I'm afraid to go alone, and the bosses are up to their asses in alligators, this week."

"Yeah, I'll help you out, Jess. What time do you want me to be here?"

"Pull up out front around six. After dinner, maybe you could take me to my car so I don't have to walk those couple of blocks in the dark."

He stood up and slung his satchel on his shoulder. "I'll definitely be here at six, but I better beat feet so I can finish in eight hours. Keep the PM and his elves off my back. Later."

"Okay, Brian. See you at six."

****

The phone on Lasky's desk rang and he picked up. "Bethlehem PD. Detective Lasky speaking."

"Detective Lasky, my name is Ethel Woods. I've been reading the papers and watching TV about these vampire killings, and I think I have some information that could help you."

"Would you like to come in and talk in person?"

"That won't be possible, Detective. I am one hundred and one years old, and I live in a nursing home in Athens, Georgia."

"Okay, Ms. Woods. What would you like to share?"

"It's a long story, one that was handed down from generation to generation in my family, but I'll try to keep it short."

"Take all the time you need, Ms. Woods."
"Please, call me Ethel."
Okay, Ethel, I'm Hyram. I'm all ears."

****

Promptly at six PM, Brian pulled up in front of the law office and tooted the horn, then waited while Jessie locked the door behind her and slid onto the passenger seat of his old Toyota. By the glow from the dome light, Brian got a pretty good look at her legs…which was odd, because he was pretty sure she had been wearing slacks earlier. Then he noticed her blouse, under her unbuttoned coat. She had changed clothes. *For me?*

He was fortunate to find a parking spot a half block from the hotel. They walked the short distance together, admiring the Christmas decorations and listening to the holiday music wafting from one of the stores. It was hard to believe that people were still out shopping; they must have felt safe. He didn't see any women walking alone, so the word about traveling at least in pairs appeared to have been taken seriously. He looked toward South Mountain and admired the Star of Bethlehem, which seemed to be hanging in the night sky above the peak. It was a wonderful illusion for everyone who ever saw it, especially from miles away.

When they stepped into the vestibule, they were greeted by more holiday music and the scent of fresh pine from the wreaths and the Christmas tree

"Brian, I have to meet the clients in their suite. I shouldn't be more than forty-five minutes, because the information I have for them is pretty cut and dried. With luck, there won't be many questions. Why don't you head to the bar and I'll meet you there when I'm finished? We could eat here, or Mama Nina's would be pretty nice. I love their garlic knots."

"Either one would be fine, Jess. We can decide when you get your butt back down here." He watched her as she walked to the elevator. Then he headed for the bar.

When one of the patrons saw Brian enter the bar, a wicked smile crossed her face.

Gloria Knecht, sporting a flaming-red wig and expensive glasses with colored lenses, muttered, "Get the fuck out. If it isn't that damn mailman!" The bar hadn't struck her as being his sort of place. She decided to stay for a while to see what he was doing.

She watched as Brian ordered a beer and casually looked around at his fellow barflies, mostly men in suits and women in dresses or pantsuits. When his gaze passed over Gloria and moved on, she knew that he hadn't recognized her.

It pleased her, hiding in plain sight. She wondered whether she should have some fun by openly flirting with Brian, but decided that it was not worth the risk.

Forty minutes later, a gorgeous blonde in a short skirt came in and walked straight over to sit down beside him. Watching them, Gloria decided that the two of them were either shacking up or would be, in the near future. She was rarely wrong about the signals, when she saw two people together like those two. Maybe she should mess with the mailman by selecting his girlfriend as the final victim. Her heightened sense of smell told her that the woman might be getting her menstrual period at the right time, but she wouldn't know for sure until the time grew closer. She'd have to keep tabs on this one.

Brian and his date had one more drink, then got up from their stools and headed out the door. Gloria followed a discreet distance behind them. When the pair walked into Mama Nina's, which wasn't very busy, she waited a few minutes and then went inside, where she secured a table within earshot.

Over the course of the meal, the two laughed and shared stories about themselves. When the check came, the woman handed the waiter her credit card.

Gloria paid her own bill and followed them out the door, where she saw them walk to the mailman's beat-up car and get in.

During their conversation in the bar, Gloria had discovered where the woman worked. She could probably find out a lot more about her potential victim by stopping by and pretending to need the services of a lawyer.

This was going to be fun.

Sunday, December 12th, 2010

Brian Miller awakened to the reality of Jessie's warm body next to him.

Never in a million years would he have thought he'd wind up in bed with this beautiful woman. The covers had made their way to the floor, and he studied her as she slept. Her angular face, slightly obscured by her shoulder-length auburn hair, was unmarred in any way. Her smooth skin had the color of soft copper, from many hours in the sun by the pool in summer time and regular tanning sessions in the winter. Though Jess's eyes were closed, he knew that they were hazel, large and expressive. She could stare you down, with either extreme intensity or incredible softness. She had full lips and, once revealed, her smile literally danced. Her smallish breasts were perfect. Although he was a breast man, he certainly ascribed to the phrase 'more than a mouthful is a waste,' and he had enjoyed a number of mouthfuls during last night's lovemaking session, which had lasted nearly three hours. Her legs were shapely, and his gaze followed them down to her dainty feet, where her nails were polished the color of a ripe apple hanging from a branch. Overall, she was amazing. He suspected he could fall in love with this lady and finally settle down for life.

He rose and strode to the bathroom, relieved himself, and washed his face and hands. He didn't want to wake her by taking a shower. Feeling a little more refreshed, he walked out to her small kitchen and began the process of making coffee. When he found the coffee, he filled the coffeemaker and waited patiently while it perked. After he had a cup and read some of the paper, he began to prepare the best omelet she might ever eat in her life. There were onions and mushrooms in the crisper and bacon in the freezer. He placed everything he needed out on the counter and started the prep work by chopping the onions, washing the mushrooms and breaking half dozen eggs in a small bowl. The only thing missing was Spam. He loved that canned meat, but he didn't eat too much of it because of the fat content.

He placed all the ingredients back in the fridge and poured another cup of coffee to sip while he finished reading the paper, which was huge, partly from the fifty or more sales flyers tucked inside, along with a special supplement concerning Gloria Knecht, the women she had killed so far, and a variety of stories relating to vampires in movies and books.

"Do I smell coffee out there, Brian? I need some really badly and I want it now."

"Yes, woman. Your wish is my command." He fixed it just the way she liked it and when he brought it to her, her attention was diverted to his penis, which was growing with each step he took.

"Christ, Brian, you look like a stallion in the pasture, ready to mount the prize mare."

He set the cup on the night stand and whinnied. She parted her legs and he slipped it inside her, making passionate love for several minutes before they both cried out in moans of pleasure.

She playfully shoved him off and reached for the cup. After a couple of sips, she sighed. "It doesn't get much better than this, does it?" She sat up. "And will I be served breakfast in bed?"

"It'll be ready in about ten minutes, if you want to take a shower."

"Have you showered yet?"

"No, because I didn't want to disturb your sleep."

She smiled lecherously. "I think I'll wait till after I've eaten and then we can save some water by showering together. We'll do our part to go green this morning."

He jumped out of bed and strolled back into the kitchen to prepare a sumptuous feast for the both of them to enjoy.

****

While Brian and Jessie were enjoying their breakfast, Hyram Lasky was working on his fourth cup of coffee and seventh cigarette while he digested the information Carl Anderson had sent to him via e-mail. Yesterday, after his conversation with Ethel, he'd phoned the Salem library and asked the librarian to see what she could find out about Amelia and any deaths or disappearances between Thanksgiving and Christmas in 1860. The woman, whose name was Harriet Beecher Stowe Madden, talked incessantly. She said it might take a little while because she'd have to contact someone at the county to go over records that dated back that far, but she'd get back to him as soon as she could.

Through the research of Carl Anderson, the phone conversation with Ethel, and whatever Harriet could dig up, Lasky was able to put together a pretty good timeline of the Christmas City vampire's murders. The only decades missing were eighteen seventy, eighteen eighty, and eighteen ninety. Librarians, police departments and local record-keepers all around the country were digging into those years.

As he scrolled to another page in the massive e-mail sent by Carl, Lasky was glad he lived in the electronic age. He couldn't imagine how long it would have taken to assemble all this information without the Internet and instant communication via phone and email, assuming it had been possible at all.

Most everything he had read so far supported the conclusion that some of slain women were experiencing their menstrual cycles when they were murdered. Lasky theorized that all of her victims in the past hundred and fifty years had been experiencing the woman's 'curse' when their lives were taken. He remembered what Sara had said about the vampire smelling their blood during those times, and it made sense. But what made her choose them instead of any other women? That would be a tough row to plow.

He picked up the phone and punched in a number.

****

Gloria Knecht needed to lay low for the next two weeks. She couldn't afford to take an extra life or two before Christmas Eve, but she was thirsty for blood. As she paced her room, she could feel her stomach tying itself in knots, and she didn't know what to do. Ever since the Godforsaken curse had begun, a hundred and fifty years ago, she'd heeded the witch's warning never to take more than five victims, and the other nine years of each decade she spent as a normal human being were absolutely wonderful, although she always regretted the necessity of taking those lives to keep her alive until she could be free.

She remembered walking back to stand outside of her aunt and uncle's house, during the blackest hours between midnight and three in the morning, and watching them comfort one another, frantic over her absence. She wanted to tell them what had happened, but she was certain they would think her a monster and have her put to death. Many times since then, Amelia had wanted to die rather than go on for the number of prescribed years, but she felt that she had been cheated out of a normal life and wanted to experience the joys and agonies associated with the aging process. She knew that now, with her face in the mind's eye of millions of people, it would be difficult to make a new start somewhere else, but she was going to live and age, come hell or high water – well, perhaps just 'high water,' since she'd been to hell and back so many times.

In 1861, she had moved to Charleston, South Carolina, where she found work as a seamstress. Going by the name Elizabeth Stanton, she could have never imagined how busy she and the women she worked with would become, sewing uniforms for the boys of the Confederacy. After the war ended, she lived for five years in San Antonio, Texas, forced to run for her life after taking her fifth victim on Christmas Eve in 1870.

There was no scarcity of women in that city, but she had a great deal of difficulty picking up the scent of one who was bleeding from her vagina. As the day grew long, she was almost ready to take anyone; her hunger was causing her head to throb. Finally, with only an hour or so to go, she saw a woman coming out from a hotel. The woman was seedy looking and smelled bad but, through the other odors, she picked up the scent of fresh blood as the woman walked past, hunched over from the pain of menstrual cramps. When she nearly fell down onto the muddy street, Elizabeth came to her rescue and steadied her. Looking around to be sure that no one else was present, she then drove her fangs into the woman's neck and sucked every drop of precious blood from her body, then laid the body down in the middle of the street.

She found she had to move to a different location every five years or so, to disguise the fact that she wasn't aging. However, in today's world, it had become much more difficult to establish a new identity, so she tried to stay longer.

Gloria had lived in Bethlehem for almost ten years, partly because the killings in 2000 had not been well-publicized. After all, who would believe a vampire was responsible? The deaths were attributed to animal attacks, or were simply dismissed as death from unknown causes.

She opened the refrigerator door and found a bottle of wine; it wasn't blood, but at least it would warm her, and alcohol did tend to abate the craving for a little while. It was going to be a long two weeks, but she was determined to stick to her course of action, although she would not remain behind closed doors for that long. She needed to get outside and enjoy the little time she had left in this city before moving on.

****

Shortly after four PM, the people Lasky had invited to his home began to show up.

The first to arrive was Brian Miller, who brought Jessie along to the dinner meeting that Lasky was hosting.

"Brian, I'm glad you could make it. Jessie, it's nice to see you again. I appreciate all the work you did for me."

Jessie simply nodded, but Brian said, "Thanks Detective. We wanted to be here to see if we can figure out how to find the vampire and end all this shit. Jess is scared to death, but I'm going to make sure nothing happens to her. I've convinced her to stay at my place until this is all over and we can get on with our lives."

Mike and Sara arrived, followed a few minutes later by Everett Gardner. Miles Steele was the last to join them. In fact, Lasky was surprised that he showed up.

Once they were all inside and seated, Lasky opened the meeting. "Dinner will be ready in an hour. Let's brainstorm before we eat.

"Yesterday I received a call from Ethel Woods. She is one hundred and one years old and lives in a nursing home. She informed me that the woman we know as Gloria Knecht was alive back in 1860 as a woman named Amelia Gibbons. Amelia disappeared while visiting her aunt and uncle in Salem, Massachusetts. I called the Salem Public Library and spoke to the librarian there, Harriet Beecher Stowe Madden." He waited for the smiles and giggles to die down. "I asked her if she could find any information about Amelia. Harriet talked my ear off, but a couple of hours later she called back to say that she had spoken with a friend who works in Public Records in Salem. Harriet said that her friend found information dating back to that period. There were five murders in Salem during the holiday season of that year, and Amelia was never heard from again. So I tend to believe that 1860 was the start of all this. I'm hoping there are people living in Salem today who have handed stories down from generation to generation. Maybe we'll come up with something that can help us find Gloria Knecht. At this point, I'll grasp at any straw that's out there."

"Hy, I have a question. Actually, several."

"The floor's yours, Jessie."

"Okay, here goes. As a paralegal, I have to cover the five points of a story in order to build our cases. First is 'who.' Well, we know who this woman is and, even better, who she may have started out as. 'What' is obvious – in this case, a vampire terrorizing our city. 'When'? Again, we know a number of whens in this case, as well as a couple of wheres. 'Why' is still up in the air, but it seems to me, since the murders only occur near the end of each ten-year period ending in the number zero, that Amelia became a vampire to satisfy some ritual."

"That's a pretty good guess, Jessie. Any other ideas about what kind of ritual may have taken place?"

"Yeah, Hyram, I think I'd like to give it a shot." Jessie looked around to make sure she had everyone's attention. "The first murders took place in Salem. I'm going to guess that a witch's curse was probably the cause."

"Oh, shit. Now we gotta deal with women on broomsticks," said Brian, who had obviously had a little too much to drink.

Sara chimed in. "I don't think there are any witches around, but I lean a little toward Jessie's theory. What else could explain a vampire? And is she the only one in existence?"

Nobody stepped on her toes, so she ventured a guess about something else. "I've been thinking about the menstrual cycle thing. I don't think it's about childbirth or anything like that, but I'm leaning toward the fact that when a woman has her period, her body is being cleansed of dead cells. Maybe the vampire needs a woman to be having her 'curse' as part of the ritual of the witch's curse."

"That's pretty good, Sar," Mike applauded.

They threw around a few more ideas, only to dismiss each of them in turn, before finally gathering in the dining room for a wonderful dinner.

After the meal, they couldn't resist brainstorming for a little bit longer, but it seemed to be getting them nowhere until Sara said, "We all know that Gloria is really good at disguises. Maybe at one point in her life she was an actress. Is there any way we can find out if any actresses went missing at the end of a decade?"

"Good thought. I'm scheduled to be on Morning America tomorrow and I'll throw that out to the people watching. Maybe we'll come up with something we can use. For now, I think we should all call it a night. My guess is that it's going to be quiet for a while, but we still have to go to our day jobs and carry on with our lives. Thank you all for coming."

Monday, December 13th, 2010

Jackie Ciamacco came on camera. "Welcome to Morning America. Our guest this morning is Detective Hyram Lasky of the Bethlehem Police Department." She turned to Lasky. "You've informed us that you and several others involved in the vampire case held a brainstorming session last night at your home. Did you come up with anything that can help find this vampire?"

Hyram Lasky came on camera and gave them a summary of the informal roundtable session. "…And the last thing we discussed was a question posed by one of our police officers, Sara Jameison. She said that, since Gloria Knecht was a master of disguise, she was curious about whether there was an instance of an actress going missing during the end of any decade. I thought about that, after they all left, and I'd like to know if a makeup specialist or an actress had been reported missing. She could have been in either capacity in the arts somewhere."

"Okay, people," Jackie said brightly, "if you have any information, please call us at the number in the crawl at the bottom of your screen. Or you can email us at the address being shown."

Gloria Knecht was watching the program. When she heard the request, she threw her coffee cup at the TV screen and jumped to her feet. "That fucking Sara." She began to pace, hoping that Jeremy Hatch wasn't watching the program. He'd call in for sure and if he did, he might be able to give them information she didn't want them to know. She should never have talked to him so often, but thirty years had passed. These days, he'd be in his seventies, if drugs or AIDS hadn't already killed the fucking faggot.

***

Jeremy Hatch thought long and hard about not dialing the phone, but he felt that he had to do it. Amanda Bronson, as she was known then, had been a miracle worker with makeup and costuming. She was the only woman he'd ever loved, in a lifetime spent as a gay male.

With a heavy sigh, he dialed the number.

When his voice came on the air, it shocked him to hear how fragile he sounded. "Good morning, Jackie. How are you/"

"I'm fine, Jeremy. And you?"

"Not so well, I'm afraid. I only have a few weeks to live, and I'm in constant pain, but this call isn't about me. Thirty years ago, I worked with a woman, Amanda Bronson. She worked in the makeup department at the Majestic Theater, here in Dover, Delaware. She disappeared around Christmas but she told me something that may give us a clue. A clue on Christmas Eve. One day when we were chatting, the subject of Christmas came up. She said that, wherever she was at Christmas time, she liked to spend some time at the highest point near her home and look at the view from there. She didn't say why she liked it so much, but I'm guessing that her plans to kill again will involve a place like that."

Hyram Lasky thanked him for the information, and then remembered the tiny Moravian star he had found at the scene of Jenna Blackman's murder. "Jackie, Joe, please excuse me. I have to get back to the station now." And with that, he stood up and walked off camera before they could even say goodbye.

****

After the two men were taken into custody, not a word was spoken by the four people in the police car as it headed back to the station. When they arrived, Mike said, "Sara, take this guy into an interview room and see what happened out there. I'll take the other one." He pointed to the tall man, who was sporting a black eye.

Once they were in the room, Mike closed the door and stared at the man for a good long time. "What the hell was that all about?"

"Hey, bro, that raghead pissed me off."

"Don't 'bro' me, you asshole. Twenty years ago, you walked out of the house. After that, I never heard a damn word from you. Mom and Dad were worried sick, but did you give them any consideration, or even think about calling them and telling them you were okay? You've gotta be the most self-centered bastard on the face of the earth. Then when I finally see you again, you're beating the crap out of a Muslim on Main Street in Bethlehem! I'm so mad, I could lock you up and throw away the key,"

Jack McGinnis stared at his brother. "You've grown up."

"Yeah, and I had to do it without you. I worshiped the ground you walked on. You were my hero. All that my friends ever talked about was the Thanksgiving Day football game when you intercepted a pass and ran it back eighty-nine yards for a touchdown to win the game. You were one of the best…and then, when you were eighteen, you walked out of the house without even a goodbye. I didn't know if you were dead or alive. And now, here you are, in cuffs, heading for at least a couple of nights behind bars. I don't get you, man."

"Mike, I had to leave. You don't remember how bad it got between Mom and me. After Dad died, she leaned on me to be the man of the house, and I couldn't deal. I wasn't ready for the kind of responsibility she wanted me to handle. Dad did everything for her, you know that, and I just wanted to be a normal teenager; hang out with my friends and play football. Getting a job for the summer wasn't on my 'things to do' list, that year."

"We needed the money, Jack. Dad left us with almost nothing, and Mom didn't know we were that close to broke. She hadn't worked for a long time because she was busy taking care for us."

Jack lowered his head for a good long while. "It was pretty rough?"

"Damn rough, Jack. Thank God Aunt Jennie was able to come through and pay off the house for us. Mom told me it was just a loan, but Jennie knew we'd never be able to pay her back. I didn't find that out until years later, but since I started working full time, I've been giving her some money each month. You know she loved the shit out of you, too, Jack."

He nodded. "Yeah, Jennie was cool. Is she doing okay?"

"She's fine, but Mom isn't doing well at all. She got cancer a couple of years ago, and it looked like she wouldn't make it. The treatments finally worked, though and she's been in remission for about eight months." When his brother didn't respond to that news, Mike looked at him. "Okay, Jack, tell me what the hell happened out there."

"I just lost it. Let me give you some of the backstory, man. Please." He looked at his brother to see if that would be okay.

Mike nodded grudgingly. "You want some coffee first?"

"No, I'm good." He looked down at his hands in silence for a long moment before saying, "So…I left home, but I really wasn't sure what I was going to do. I had about a thousand bucks saved up and I knew that wouldn't last very long. I was living in Philly, sharing a three-bedroom apartment with a couple of guys I met in high school. After graduation, they wanted a little adventure, so they took off for the bright lights of the big city. I had their number and gave them a call and we got together. I worked with them in a band for about a year, playing drums, making a little money, but when Desert Storm broke out, all three of us, drunk as skunks, headed for the recruiting office and signed up. We wanted to save the world from the Iraqis."

"You joined the Army?"

"No, man. We went right to the big time and became Marines."

At that, Mike smiled for the first time since seeing his brother again.

"Anyway, they sent us to Parris Island, and that's where I found out I wasn't as tough as I thought. By that time, though, there was no turning back. I was in pretty good shape, but let me tell you, Mike, Marine boot camp beats the crap out of you. I actually excelled there and they sent me on to sniper school. Eight years ago, I picked off an enemy soldier at two thousand yards."

"How long were you a Marine, Jack?"

"Once a Marine, always a Marine, buddy." He smiled sadly. "I'm still active. In fact, I'm headed to Afghanistan after the holidays…but I might be in some deep shit, after dropping that raghead today."

"You're a fuckin' lifer? Unbelievable! Look, Jack, I'm going to talk to my partner, and then I have to see a guy. I gotta lock you in the room, man."

"No sweat, Brother. Just don't leave me hanging forever."

Mike left him there and knocked on the door of the other interview room, then walked in. "Sara, can you step out here a couple of minutes? I need to talk to you."

Once they were in the hall, she asked, "What's up?"

"What's that guy have to say about the fight?"

"Well, he's a little hard to understand, but from what I could make out, the big white guy saw him on the street and went ballistic, pushing him, calling him names. He got one good shot in on your guy, but then your guy started beating the crap out of him. I guess we were lucky to happen by when we did. That bastard in your room must be a raving lunatic."

"He's not only is a lunatic, he's a Marine sniper. And, Sara, that lunatic is my brother."

Her jaw dropped. "Your brother! Oh, Mike, that's not good at all."

"No, it's not, but there's a chance we can use his help to get rid of Gloria Knecht. Talk to your man and see if he'll take money not to charge Jack with assault or anything. I know I'm way out of line here, but I don't know what else to do."

"Okay. Give me a couple of minutes to see what I can do." She grinned. "I think he likes me."

Mike waited in the hall, trying not to pace.

Three minutes later, she came back out. "You probably won't like this, but he wants ten thousand dollars not to press charges, and he wants all his injuries taken care of financially."

"Man, that's a lot of money…but I think between Jack and I we can swing it. The medical shit is going to be tough, but I'm gonna go talk to Lasky and see what we can do."

****

Jessie Sterling was working alone at the law office, since both attorneys had to be in court.

An elegantly dressed middle-aged woman walked in and sat down, clearly prepared to wait until Jessie, who was in the midst of an animated phone conversation, could speak with her.

Jessie wrapped up her call and hung up the phone. "Good morning. May I help you?"

The woman strode to a chair beside Jessie's desk and sat down. "I certainly hope so, Miss…"

"Sterling. Jessie Sterling. Please call me Jessie."

"Thank you, Jessie. I'm Francis Cunningham and I have a problem. That husband of mine has upset me for the last time, and I want out."

"I'm sorry to hear that, Mrs. Cunningham, but we don't handle divorce cases. I can give you the name of a good family law attorney. She's a barracuda and always does the very best she can for her clients. Her name is Melissa Finley and she has an office on the other side of town."

"Oh. I see. Sorry for disturbing you, dear. I assumed that every lawyer took on divorces. Could you please give me Mrs. Finley's phone number and address? I'll contact her immediately."

"Certainly, Mrs. Cunningham. It would be my pleasure." She jotted the information on a card and handed it to the woman, who then rose and strolled out the door.

Jessie got up from her desk and watched the woman get into a black late model Lexus. Then she went back to her desk and picked up the phone.

When Brian saw Jessie's name and number appear on his cell phone, he answered. "Hi, honey, how are you?"

"Brian, you won't believe this, but Gloria Knecht was just here in my office."

"Oh, my God! Did she try to do anything to you? I can come right over –"

"No need, honey, I'm okay. She was dressed to the nines, driving a black Lexus. I knew her immediately from her eyes. You can disguise anything you want, but eyes never change. I'm pretty sure she didn't catch on that I knew who she was, but I think she was here to get a closer look at me."

"Why do you think that?"

"Well, she had contact with you more than once, so maybe she saw us together somewhere" Jess pounded the desk with her fist. "Shit! Brian, she did see us together? When we were sitting in the bar at the Hotel Bethlehem, she was there as well. That night she was a young redhead, but because she was wearing red tinted glasses, I didn't see her eyes. Then later, I noticed her at Mama Nina's. I think she was stalking us."

"Yeah, that could be true, but how did she know your name and where you worked."

"I'm only guessing that from the fiction we read and see on the screen, vampires are supposed to have very acute hearing."

"Did you get her license number?"

"Just a partial and I'm going to call it in, but I'd bet the car was either stolen or rented."

"Maybe the cops can find her and put her under surveillance. If they find out where she's staying, it might be easy to get to her and destroy her before she kills anyone else."

"Okay, Brian, I'm hanging up now and calling the police."

****

"…so that's the whole story, Detective. What do you think?"

"I think it can be done, but I'll have to see the chief. This may take a little time."

"Whatever it takes. Jack's willing to wait, because the last thing he needs is this kind of incident on his record. He can retire in another two years, if he can get out from under this."

Mike and Sara let their respective guys stew for another hour while they waited for word from Lasky. Finally, he showed up in person and said, "It's a deal. The chief will go for anything that might help us kill the vampire. We made a few discreet inquiries, and he's impressed with your brother's shooting ability. Let me get the paper work started. With luck, we'll have these two guys out of here before dinner."

"Thanks, Detective. I'll go tell Jack."

****

By the time Mike finished his explanation, Jack looked stunned. "It's a lot of money, Mike, but it's definitely worth it if it means not getting thrown out of the Corps before I can retire." Jack smiled and his posture improved rapidly as he realized that he wouldn't have a blemish on his record, and that his retirement would be secured if he didn't screw up again.

A few hours later, when Mike's shift was finally finished, he returned to the room one last time, to pick up his brother. "Okay, Jack, it's done. Time for us to go see Mom."

Jack nodded and Mike finally relented and gave him a hug.

****

When Lasky heard the latest news about the vampire being sighted, he began to believe that she could really be caught or killed soon. . They didn't have her yet, but there were a lot of cops out there in plain clothes, plus a lot of detectives as well. They were searching a broad area, and had to get really lucky, but he was praying hard that she would be spotted. The idea of shadowing her was appealing, but they'd have to be very careful and not be spotted watching her or anything could happen.

Less than an hour later, word reached him that Gloria Knecht, still in her disguise as an affluent middle-aged woman, had been spotted going into Margo's Accents on Third Street. The plainclothes officer that saw her was told to remain vigilant but out of sight, so that Gloria wouldn't be tipped off in any way that she was being watched.

Several police cars were soon in place, ready to stop traffic and establish a cordon around that block. Three plainclothes detectives took up surveillance across the street from the store, deep in the shadows of doorways, biding their time.

****

Gloria was in the midst of admiring the amazing array of jewelry and high-end merchandise when she began to feel as if she was being watched. Trying to appear casual, she took a quick glance through the front window, and spotted a man staring hard at the store front. He didn't seem to see her, but she was filled with a sudden conviction that, if she wanted to get out of there alive, she would have to act quickly before the whole fucking Bethlehem PD could gather out there, ready to capture or kill her. She had no intention of letting that happen.

She had been concerned after she left the lawyers' office, when she saw Jessie come to the door, but getting close to the young woman had been essential, to see if she might be the one. Gloria hadn't smelled any fresh blood, but she would arrange to be in her near presence again on Christmas Eve morning, so that she would know for sure. At one time, she had hoped that the final woman she would ever have to kill would be Sara Jameison, until Sara told her that she hadn't had her period in six months, and that even taking estrogen wasn't working. That definitely ruled Sara out.

Meanwhile, if Jessie could not be the one, she would simply have to find some other woman who fit the bill in time for the ritual killing to be performed.

As she pretended to browse again, a plainclothes cop strolled into the building. He wandered into the store a bit aimlessly, like a guy forced to shop for his wife or girlfriend, and even Gloria had to admit the guy was playing the role quite well, but she knew it wouldn't be long before he tried to corner her.

Instead, she grabbed a beautiful crystal vase from a glass shelf and broke it. Satisfied that it had created a disturbance that gained everyone's attention, Gloria locked an arm around a nearby shopper. "Everyone stay back. I'm leaving here or this girl will be a bloody mess on your beautiful floor." For the benefit of those staring at her, she bared her fangs, inciting a stampede of shoppers as they trampled over one another to get the hell out of there.

Within minutes, the only people left in the building were Gloria, her hostage and the cop.

Gloria stared hard at the man, who remained outwardly calm.

"What do you want? I don't want to see that woman hurt, although I'd love to put a stake through your heart, you bitch."

She laughed in his face. "And what makes you think that would kill me? Fuckin' books and movies is what. You people have no clue how I can be destroyed, and I doubt if any of you will find out in time."

"Okay, so what do you want?"

"I want out of here, with no cops on our tail. You're driving. If you behave, I'll let you and the woman live. How does that sound, sport?"

"We can do that. I'll bring my car to the front door and tell everyone to back off."

"You tell them that if I even think I see a cop, I'll kill the woman first and then you. Got it?"

"I got it. Don't go anywhere."

Once he was clear of the building, Lasky grabbed him. "What the hell did you go in there for?"

"I thought maybe I'd be able to get the drop on her and end this shit, right here and now."

"Okay, I'll buy that, but since she made you almost immediately, a woman's life is now at stake. I assume you're out here because she wants something."

The officer told him what Gloria wanted. "Just make sure no one is tailing us or we're dead ducks."

"And what about when you get where she wants you to go? Do you really think she'll let you and the woman come out of it alive?"

He shrugged. "I don't know, boss, but we don't have much of a choice, do we?"

Lasky shook his head. "Okay, Miles. Go get your car."

A few minutes later, Detective Miles Steele stopped the car on the street at the front door of Margot's.

Gloria Knecht emerged, keeping the woman in a tight chokehold, waving the broken vase menacingly at the crowd on the street as she bared her fangs again for good measure. Cops were at every intersection, stopping traffic to allow Steele's car to travel freely.

Once he was on 378 northbound, Gloria released the woman, who quickly slid to the other side of the car and cowered against the door, her eyes were wide with fright.

They took a right on Eighth Avenue, a left on Schoenersville Road, then a right on Golf Course Road. As soon as they were beside the Bethlehem Municipal Golf Course, Gloria told him to stop.

When he did, she leaned over to him and whispered, "Lasky knows all about your lifestyle, Detective Steele. You're going down." Then she hopped out of the car and raced across the golf course, quickly disappearing from sight.

Miles leaned over the seat to look at the woman huddled there. "Are you alright, ma'am?"

She shook her head. "I don't think I'll ever be alright again, but at least I'm alive," she said, and managed a weak smile.

"You got that right," Miles said, and called in, telling Lasky where Gloria Knecht had demanded to be dropped off and assuring him that he and the woman were okay and on their way back to the station where she was checked out by a paramedic and then wrote her statement.

****

After escorting her home, Miles Steele headed back to the station. His insides were as tight as they could get, his hands had begun to shake, and, Lasky knew and he was going to be sent to prison for the rest of his life.

Twenty minutes later, he walked into his empty house and pulled out a bottle of Jim Beam. After drinking half of it, he put his service weapon to the side of his head and pulled the trigger.

****

That evening, Mike McGinnis and his brother Jack had a long talk with their mother. She was angry with Jack for walking out of their lives all those years ago but, as most mothers would do, she welcomed him back with open arms. Her son was home. Soon, however, he would be needed to rid the country of the vampire

****

Detective Lasky was getting ready for bed when the phone rang. He listened for several minutes, and then dropped the receiver back into its cradle. Miles Steele had killed himself, and now Lasky would never find out who had been heading up the ring of thieves stealing drugs and precious gems. Of course, that didn't matter very much right now. They had a vampire to kill, and she would be killed or he'd die trying.

****

Sara Jameison had no trouble falling asleep. She had taken a couple of Tylenol PMs an hour before bed, and she drifted off immediately. Near dawn, however, nightmares rose up to haunt her. In time, they faded, leaving no memory behind, but she woke up hours later, feeling crappy.

****

By the time Brian and Jessie had hashed over the events of the day, Jessie was convinced that she hadn't seen the last of Gloria Knecht. She was sure that, no matter what she did to protect herself, the vampire would find a way to get close to her and intended to kill her horribly. She cried herself to sleep, while Brian held on to her and stayed awake for most of the night.

Tuesday, December 14th, 2010

Gloria Knecht woke from a restless sleep and looked at the clock: four forty-seven AM.

She sat up on the bed and stretched. This, the final year of the curse, was proving to be most difficult. Her pursuers had gotten much too close for comfort, and yesterday's experience was one of the worst she'd ever had.

When she'd seen Miles Steele walking into Margot's, it had taken her by surprise. She had never thought that he would be the one to nearly end her existence. The guy actually had a pair, even though she thought at previous meetings that he was only talking a tough game.

After he dropped her off beside the golf course, she did have a moment when she considered killing him and the frightened woman in the backseat of the car, but decided it would serve no purpose in helping to lift the curse, and so she let them go. She thought that telling Steele that Lasky knew about his activities would have messed up his mind plenty.

As she ran across the golf course, she felt a renewed energy. There was something about running that really was therapeutic for both body and mind. And it served her purpose well, since she needed to get back to her room in a hurry. The cops would be all over the area, ready to hunt her down like a wild animal. Of course, within the time frame when she had to take blood, she was a wild animal. But it was worth it, to be able to live a normal life for the other nine years and eleven months of each decade.

'Borrowing' a car from the motel parking lot, she hot-wired it and began her drive into the city. As she cruised down 378, she looked up at the Moravian Star on top of the mountain, marveling at its brightness. She had read somewhere that a new type of bulb had been installed to increase the wattage, making the star even more spectacular. The first day she had set foot in the city, she'd been enthralled by the magic of the Star, which had been erected in the 1930s, when Bethlehem was first dubbed 'The Christmas City.' People from all over the world came to stroll down Main Street and gaze upon buildings that had been in existence since Bethlehem's birth in 1741.

She parked her car on Main Street and got out to take a walk and think. No one was in her field of vision, so she cautiously walked down toward the Hotel Bethlehem. Moments later she picked up the sound of a car and stepped into a doorway until the vehicle passed.

Gloria looked at the streetlights, marveling at the beauty of their Christmas decorations, and she longed for the days of her youth. She was certain she would have had a wonderful life, rich in friends and relations, and probably a family of her own, had she not been taken by the witch on that day so long ago.

She stayed in Salem that year until Christmas Day and then she found a new place to live in New York. She had never returned home and had no idea how long her parents and siblings lived. She was afraid to go back, even for a short time; because she didn't want to take the chance that she would tell family members what had happened to her.

After this, the curse would be lifted. Then, finally, she could start all over. She would fall in love with a great man, have kids, and grow old while enjoying all of the wonderful things that families did together. She realized that she would probably have to live overseas, in her new life, which was to begin in less than two weeks.

Excited by the prospect, she smiled and nodded at a maintenance man who was stabbing litter from the sidewalk with a spear-like tool. He didn't seem happy to be out on a cold day but, like any human, he had a job to do for as many years as he had to do it. He simply nodded back and went about his work.

She sat down at a table in front of a restaurant and lit a cigarette. She'd have to stop smoking once she was completely human again because she wouldn't take any chances with her life by opening up the possibility of getting cancer. She had seen what cancer could do to a person, during a period of time back in the eighties when she worked at a hospital as an aide. It had been really a good year and a half because, when she felt the need for blood, the blood storage facility was a snap to break into. The head of the department pulled his hair out whenever a bag or two was discovered missing, and all the employees were questioned, but they never found out what had happened to the missing blood or who had taken it.

She lit up another cigarette and resumed her walk, retracing the route she had driven. The car would shortly be reported stolen, and she didn't need to be seen in a stolen vehicle, this close to the end of her efforts. She drew the hood of her sweatshirt tight against her face, hiding more of her features.

Back on 378, crossing the Hill to Hill Bridge, she turned once again to look at the Star of Bethlehem, and decided that the final act of her killing spree would end forever, as she bathed in the light at the base of the Star.

As her walk turned into a jog, and then a full run, she thought about the time fifty years ago when she had nearly been captured, just a few days after her one hundredth anniversary of being a vampire.

****

She was having difficulty finding the scent of a woman having her menstrual cycle, and her need for a victim was tempting her to making rash decisions. In a bar, she finally found the scent she was looking for, and struck up a conversation with a woman who had visibly had too much to drink and was ripe for the taking.

Gloria offered to help her get back to her car and drive her home, but the woman was adamant that she could drive herself, thank you. She did, however, accept the offer for assistance in finding her car. "I guess I'm a little woozy," the woman said, meekly "But I'm sure I'll be okay once I take in a few good breaths of fresh air."

As they approached the car, Gloria's need became unbearable. She pulled the woman into a side alley. When the woman saw her benefactor's fangs growing inside her mouth, her screams grew louder, until Gloria stifled them by covering her open mouth with a gloved hand. "Shh,' she said, "This will only hurt for a moment. Then you will drift to sleep forever."

The woman's eyes bulged as the vampire's fangs sank through her flesh. Her heart raced as her precious blood was transferred into

Gloria, swallow by swallow. She began her death throes, clinging to life, unwilling to die without a fight, but she became weaker with each passing moment, finally expiring as the vampire took a final swallow.

Satisfied, energized, Gloria gently laid the woman on the street. Rising to leave the scene, she froze when she saw that the alley was blocked by two police officers. When they saw what she was, they drew their guns and fired.

Gloria had never been shot before and she was certain that she could be killed in this manner but, when the bullets passed through her body, she remained on her feet. There was a little pain, but it lasted only momentarily.

The two officers looked stunned, but each continued to fire as Gloria calmly walked toward them. "Ain't life a bitch when bullets don't work, my friends?"

She delivered the back of her right hand to one cop's face, and the strength of her blow lifted him off his feet and sent him flying through the air to land on a trash can fifteen feet away. The other cop began to run, but he had only taken a couple of steps when she lifted him off his feet and tossed him like a rag doll to land next to his partner. She casually strolled over to them and listened for heartbeats. The second cop was still alive, so she snapped his neck.

Gloria looked around for any other witnesses, but no one else was nearby. Satisfied, she simply walked away, full of the life she needed to survive until the curse called for another victim's blood.

****

Arriving back at the motel, Gloria had to smile. The police department was being efficient as hell about interviewing a man who was standing there in his pajamas and robe. He pointed to his empty parking space, his mouth going a mile a minute. Gloria slipped her hands into the little pocket of her sweatshirt, lowered her head and walked right past them and into the motel lobby.

Back in her room, she stripped and took a hot shower, then sat down on the bed and pulled a leather briefcase from under it. Opening the lid, she pulled out a sharp wooden stake. Many times in the past, she had been tempted to pierce her own heart, just to see if that was a way she could be killed. Now, with the cops getting closer to her each day, she needed to know,

She placed the tip of the stake against her skin. When it penetrated, drawing some blood, she felt very little pain. She was actually surprised she felt any, since bullets had caused no pain at all when she had been hit.

Slowly guiding the point closer and closer to her heart, she felt little, and when she finally pierced the body's largest muscle, she smiled, pushing it in even farther, until the point passed through her back. Gloria was elated. Here was yet another method of death that wouldn't work.

She pulled the stake back out and still marveled at how quickly she healed from the wound.

A long time ago, she had been cornered inside a church. The preacher stabbed her with a silver cross that had very little effect on her.

Fire was another story. Another time, she was living in an apartment building that had caught on fire. During her escape, she had felt the flames lick her arm, and that had hurt a lot. Once she was out of the building, however, she had quickly healed.

Gloria also could not try to behead herself, so that was a possibility, but there'd be no way in hell anyone would be able to get close enough to her to use a sword or other weapon capable of removing a head.

She felt positive that on Christmas Eve, the one-hundred-and-fifty-year curse would come to an end, and she could hardly wait.

****

Brian Miller went to work, but he was preoccupied with concern about Jessie's safety. Three times, the vampire had gotten close to him. The odds were, if it happened again, that one of them would not leave alive.

After punching in and walking out to do his vehicle check, he lit a cigarette, but put it out almost immediately. It tasted like shit. Maybe that meant that the Chantix he had started taking less than a week ago was starting to work. He hoped he could get Jessie on the program, too; he wanted them to have long lives together. He was pretty sure she was 'the one,' but only more time together would seal that assumption.

When he returned to the office and got to his case, he was dismayed by the amount of mail that was already on the floor and the ledge: four tubs of flats, two sets of holiday circulars and a tray and a half of letter mail, predominantly Christmas cards. Casing all of that would probably keep him inside for an additional forty-five minutes, even without putting in all the bulk flats. The circs were dated and, as usual, had arrived late. Both would have to go today.

With a sigh, he put in the ear buds and turned on his iPod. Music always helped him get through the drudgery of casing mail, and he especially needed it today; even if he skipped lunch, he'd still probably finish around dark. He'd be hungry as a bear when the day was done, but Jessie was going to make chili. That, along with a salad, bread, and a couple of Yuenglings would fill him up in no time. He smiled recalling the time his cousin called Yuengling vitamin Y.

****

On Morning America, footage of the vampire and her hostage getting into the detective's car was shown. They still didn't know about Miles Steele's death, but that information couldn't be held from the media for too long and it would be all over the news by noon.

They also reported on the tragic deaths of three high school students who had been shot only two blocks from an Allentown High School. They showed the local news clips of interviews with spokesmen from the Allentown Police Department, and with security officers installed inside the buildings a number of years ago.

After resuming their normal discussions about what the president was doing, and interviews with leaders from both the right and the left, they rounded out the program with live footage of a fire that had already consumed seven row homes in Easton, Pennsylvania, a town not far from Bethlehem.

When the program was over, the stars sauntered out into the crowd on the library patio, greeting as many of the audience as possible before being whisked away in their limos. Ken Glass went in a separate car because he was going to sign books at the Moravian Book Shop. When he arrived he was greeted by almost a hundred people outside and half that many already lined up to meet the author of <u>Freaky America</u>.

****

Members of the Bethlehem Police Department were researching everything they could find about the previous vampire slayings, but they still couldn't come up with a plan to facilitate Gloria Knecht's destruction.

Lasky had a phone conversation with Carl Anderson to see if the team he had assembled had come up with anything they could use to track her down and end the current reign of terror.

Brian and Sara were on routine patrol, and it was a quiet day both inside and outside the vehicle. Both officers were mentally dealing with concerns they were unwilling to share with each other. To break the awkward silence, Sara asked, "How did it go with Jack and your mom?"

Mike smiled. "It went pretty well. Mom was glad to see her other son but she really let him have it for never calling or writing. She'd had no idea whether he was alive or dead. He explained why he had to leave, and why he went in the military, but he never told her he was a sniper. I guess he figured she really didn't need to know how often he was in harm's way in his nineteen-year career."

"Did either of you mention how you found each other again?"

"No, Sara. Mom would have been really bummed if she'd known that he beat the crap out of a random guy. That deal is dead and buried, as far as I'm concerned." He glanced over at her. "You okay? You really looked tired when you came in, this morning."

She nodded and took a sip from her coffee cup. "I had an awful night. I dreamed that Gloria kidnapped me and took me up to the Star of Bethlehem. I kept fighting her off, all the way from the car to the Star, but she was strong. When she ripped the lock off the gate and we got to within a couple of yards of the Star – and it's fuckin' huge, Mike – she made me look down at the city, bright lights glowing all over. The view was amazing. After we'd watched the city for a couple of minutes, she grabbed my hair and exposed my neck. I felt her hot breath, and then the tips of her fangs entered my neck, so I screamed – and that's when I woke up."

"My God, Sara. That would have scared the crap out of me, too. Don't worry. Jack and I won't let her get anywhere near you, between now and Christmas Eve."

"You can't be my bodyguard, Mike. I'm a big girl, and a cop to boot. I can take care of myself."

"Not going to happen, kiddo. We're going to be near you as much as possible. And when you're inside your apartment, we want you to stay put. If you really need to go out for any reason, call one of us."

At that moment, she honestly wished she could once again have a relationship with a man, but no matter how nice the guy was there was always going to be mistrust and nervousness. Of course, she sure as hell hadn't gotten very far with Gloria. Her mind was really screwed up. Maybe, after this was all over, she'd ask Mike out and see what happened... *Wait a minute, you idiot. He's still married!*

But she was certain that was going to change.

****

On Main Street, shops closed their doors at the end of the day, and shoppers headed home, to one of the local restaurants or bars, or the Brew Works. Although there was still a high level of fear, most people were learning to deal with it, except for women who were due to experience their menstrual cycles on Christmas Eve. Many of those women decided to visit relatives outside the city, or at least rent a room for that one night, outside of the city.

By eleven PM, even the bars had shut down for lack of customers. There was a lot of grumbling by the owners of those establishments, wanting to get business back to normal.

Would that ever happen again?

Wednesday, December 15th, 2010

Early in the morning, Jack McGinnis began the daunting task of finding the highest spots overlooking Bethlehem, to determine where he could hide to get a clean shot at the vampire. He called a couple of his friends who had been in the Corps and were still available to help Jack out, when needed.

First, he went to the Star of Bethlehem on South Mountain. There, he found a perfect spot, roughly seventy-five yards away, which offered a clear one-hundred-and-eighty-degree view of the Star and the surrounding area, where someone would be afforded the best view of the city.

After that, he drove back into town and selected a building several blocks from the Hotel Bethlehem. Because of the city's topography, this building actually rose a little higher than the majestic hotel. It was always better to be above a target than below it, because of the drop of the bullet. Besides, he needed to see the entire target in order to know exactly where the hostage would be; positioning himself below them wouldn't give him the best view.

Jack examined a few other possible places where the vampire might take her victim, but ruled them all out because they weren't as high as the Star and the hotel. When he imagined himself as her, the places just didn't feel right.

Everyone involved in the mission to destroy Gloria Knecht wanted a piece of her, but Jack was convinced he would need professional shooters to get the job done, not a bunch of city cops and detectives, a mailman and a paralegal. Keeping them out of harm's way when the time came wasn't going to be easy. He didn't blame them, but he was afraid they wouldn't remain sufficiently calm under the pressure. He was pretty sure there would only be one chance to get her.

****

Mike and Sara were called to the scene of a disturbance near the one hundred block of East Broad Street.

Arriving, they had to work themselves through a crowd of people. When they saw what they had been called in to investigate, they almost laughed, but it really wasn't funny.

A young woman had chained herself to a steel fence and was sitting on the pavement, Indian style. In front of her was a handwritten sign that read: GLORIA KNECHT PLEASE TAKE ME. I DON'T WANT TO LIVE ANYMORE.

Mike shook his head. "Don't tell me the crazies in town are going to start this kind of shit," he muttered to Sara.

"I don't know. I'll talk to her and see why she's so willing to die."

"Okay, have at it. I'll move these people along while you work your magic."

As Mike worked to disperse the onlookers, Sara hunkered down beside the woman, who Sara figured to be in her early twenties. She was nicely dressed, and Sara noticed a brand-new Beamer parked nearby, with its trunk and passenger door wide open.

Sara touched the woman's hair and asked, "What's the matter, honey?"

The woman began to cry. "Chad broke our engagement. I just can't live without him. We've been together for five years and I love him so much…"

Sara put an arm around the weeping woman. "I'm Sara Jameison. What's your name, sweetie?"

"I'm a Sarah, too! Sarah Moore."

"Do you live nearby?"

"No. Quakertown."

When Mike heard her name and where she lived he called it in to see what else they could find out about her."

"I understand. I've had broken relationships in my life. It isn't easy." *Especially when one of your lovers turns out to be a vampire...*

The woman recoiled. "Understand?" she echoed belligerently. "How the hell could you understand? You cops think you know all the fucking answers!"

Sara tried to calm her, wondering if the woman was bipolar. They'd have their work cut out for them, trying to contain the situation until someone arrived to cut the locks off…

Her heart sank as she saw an ANN van arriving. A cameraman hurried out, along with a young man holding a boom mic – the last thing she needed in an already volatile situation. "Mike," she called out, "keep 'em back."

Mike positioned himself on the sidewalk between the television people and the two women. "No farther, guys."

The two men stood in the street, clearly determined not to miss out on an opportunity for a story. Other cops joined Mike in trying to keep the onlookers at bay, with limited success.

When a metro bus stopped a little way down the street, several of the passengers got out and walked up the street to join the growing crowd of gawkers. Gloria Knecht was amused when she spotted the woman and her sign, as well as Sara Jameison and her partner, Mike McGinnis. She worked her way to a good vantage point in front of a building just up the street, laughing inwardly as she once again hid in plain sight, her only disguise the hooded sweatshirt she frequently wore when in the city. She listened hard, easily picking up the conversation between the two women.

Sara continued to stroke Sarah's hair, comforting her. "That's true, I can't really understand what you're going through right now, but I do understand that you're hurting. If you tell me about it, maybe we can resolve your issue. You're much too young to die, especially as the victim of a vampire."

Sarah sighed. "Three months ago, I didn't get my period, and I was sure I was pregnant. When Chad came home that night, I told him, and he just flipped out on me." She started to cry, and it took a while for her to compose herself. "He told me he wasn't ready for kids, and didn't know if he would ever want to raise a child in this economy. He just kept babbling on and on. I couldn't believe it. I thought he loved me so much that my pregnancy wouldn't be any barrier at all."

A police officer approached, carrying a bolt cutter, and Sarah shrank away from him.

"It's okay, Sarah. No one's going to hurt you. We just want to help," Sara said as the cop began to cut the lock. "What happened after that?"

"He threw me out the house and told me it was over. A month later, I got my period! I was so happy I wasn't pregnant that I called him and told him the news, but he still didn't want to see me again." After the lock was cut and her chains removed, she stood up. "I went to see him this morning, though," she told Sara as she picked up her large purse.

"Is he going to take you back?"

"He can't." She wrapped one arm around Sara, drew a .45 caliber pistol out of her bag, and placed the barrel to Sara's head. "Because I killed him. And now I have to shoot you, too. That way, one of those cops will kill me, and my suffering will be over." With four guns pointed at her, she said loudly, "If you don't want her dead, move back, now."

The cops moved back into the street, and as Sarah watched them, Mike saw her looking at his fellow officers, but not at him. He slowly took his gun from the holster and figured there was only one way to save his partner's life. He cried out, "Let her go."

As Sarah looked his way, Sara wriggled out of her grasp, just enough for the gun to be pointed elsewhere, and not at her head.

Mike fired. The bullet hit Sarah in her right eye and exploded out the back of her head. Her body tumbled to the sidewalk.

Pandemonium broke out, with some onlookers taking off and others hitting the ground. The cameraman kept shooting, but the mic guy lost whatever was in his stomach. The other cops immediately attempted to control the crowd.

Mike just looked away.

When he looked across the street, he spotted a woman in a hooded sweatshirt who was laughing like crazy. Raising his gun, he yelled, "Gloria! I know it's you."

Many of the onlookers turned toward her when Mike called her name.

Gloria opened the drawstring of her hood and pulled it from her face and hair, allowing everyone to see who she was. An audible gasp could be heard from many of the people. She called out, "Bring it on, Mikey."

Mike fired.

He saw the round hit her in the chest, but she didn't drop. He fired again, and again hit her in the chest.

She waved and took off down the street, proving to Mike and the other witnesses that bullets would not take down a vampire.

Shaken, Sara made her way over to him and hugged him tight. "You saved my life, Mike. I owe you big time."

Mike continued to watch Gloria retreating, chased by several men. They disparately tried to catch her, but she scooted down an alley at an unbelievable speed.

The men came back several minutes later, shrugging their shoulders. Gloria won again.

Later, at the station, Mike filled out the lengthy paperwork and then was interviewed by Detective Lasky, but it was clear that nobody in their right mind was going to levy any punishment against him for firing his weapon.

After their shift was over, Mike followed Sara to her house, and then went home to his wife. He was bone tired, and it was only then that his hands began to shake.

Thursday, December 16th, 2010

As was his norm, Roy Clayton was up by five AM. Even on his four day weekends he rarely slept much later than six. He went to the bathroom, checked his weight, and strolled out to the kitchen to make coffee. He knew he could have a nice breakfast this morning because he had dropped another pound. Since getting on Weight Watchers six months ago he was down thirty-two pounds and now only had to weigh in once a month.

Riley, his stepson's dog, was at his feet and Roy began the ritual of talking to him. He wished Riley could talk; maybe he'd even have a solution to end the vampire madness. Dogs were extremely smart.

Roy poured a cup of coffee, walked into the den, sat down and turned on the computer. While waiting for his computer to boot up, he looked at his watch and was startled when he noticed the date: December 16th. On that date in 1970, forty years earlier, he had come home from Vietnam. The memories took hold, superseding everything else that was tumbling around in his head: his last day in country, the flight to California and on to Philadelphia, spending the day at his cousin's apartment and then being driven home; the greeting he'd gotten from his family, and the many hours spent drinking afterward. Then, finally, nearly thirty-six hours of glorious sleep...

He shook his head. Could forty years really have gone by in the virtual blink of an eye?

When he clicked on Internet Explorer and brought up his homepage, he read the story about the previous day's shootings in Bethlehem, and was stunned. Vampire authors often took liberties with the way an undead human could be killed. Personally, he thought a bullet would do the job, no matter what he dreamed up for his fiction. But if a bullet couldn't take her down, a stake to the heart probably couldn't do it, either. He smiled, suspecting he had been right when he wrote his novel. He doubted if they'd be able to drown the bitch, and they'd never be able to set her on fire, since she'd probably be holding on to a hostage for dear life. No way would anyone be able to get close enough to her to take off her head with a sword or an axe, either. So how the hell could she be killed?

He pushed those thoughts to the back burner of his brain, and turned it to low. He wanted to write his daily quota of two thousand words, especially since he'd been contacted by a publisher that wanted to rerelease his two books under their flag. He was in the process of working out a deal with them for a book a year, with a very nice advance in the offing.

A couple of hours, five cups of coffee and only seven hundred words into a new chapter later, a thought struck him. After mulling it over briefly, he dialed a number.

"Bethlehem PD. Detective Lasky speaking."

Roy reintroduced himself and shared his idea with Lasky.

"I don't know, Roy. That might work but, after yesterday, I can't be absolutely sure."

"I agree, but what else can we do? I don't want to see anyone else murdered, and I don't think you do, either."

"I don't. Let me make some calls and get a few more opinions. Maybe you've struck gold, but..." His voice trailed off and he hung up the phone.

With a sigh, Roy tried to refocus on the day's chapter, content at least that he had done what he could.

****

Lasky sat for a few minutes, digesting the idea. Then he set the wheels in motion by calling Jack McGinnis to see if Clayton's theory was indeed possible.

Jack listened closely to the idea germinated by the writer, then said, "Hyram, that just might work. Let me get a couple of prototypes made. I'll get out to a range tomorrow and try them out."

"Do that. Then let me know if you still think it's possible."

"Will do. Talk to you tomorrow."

****

After the call, intrigued, Jack went down into his mother's basement, carrying his metal case. It held the tools he needed, and he set to work, hollowing out the explosive tips of several bullets. He worked them out to the thinnest shell he could possibly make; just enough for the bullet to still hold together in spite of the incredible heat it would be subjected to when fired. Next, he took the bottle of water and inserted a few drops into the hollowed out points, then sealed the bottoms of the tips into the casing, relieved when he saw that the sealing process worked. All he had to do now was fire them into a couple of pumpkins and check out the results.

****

Sara took a good hot shower, feeling dirty and stupid over being so unprepared for what had happened to her yesterday. She never wanted to get that close to death again. Maybe it was time to consider resigning from the police force and getting a regular day job. Having the day off gave her a lot of time to think – maybe too much time.

The phone rang and she picked up. "Hello?"

"Hi. It's Mike. How are you doing, partner?"

She sighed. "I feel like such an idiot. I should have known better than to let her get that close to me."

"You were just trying to help her though a difficult experience."

"But I came so close to dying! If you hadn't managed to kill her when you did…" Her throat tightened, and she began to cry.

When she finally got herself under control again, Mike said, "I couldn't see any other way to save your life."

A shaky sigh vibrated through her. "I'll always be indebted to you, Mike. You're a terrific partner, and a great friend." She hesitated, then added, "I wish you weren't married because I'd love it if you could come over tonight."

It was Mike's turn to sigh. "I'm flattered. And I do have feelings for you…but now isn't the time. Maybe after this vampire shit is done with. Who knows?"

"Yeah, who knows?" She searched for a way to defuse the tension of the moment. "Hey, I wanted to ask you something. How did you figure out that the woman you shot at was Gloria, before you called out her name?

"I saw her laughing. That was the first clue. And when I saw her stare right through me, I was positive. I still can't believe she didn't go down, with two bullets in her chest. I'm lucky that the ricochets off the wall behind her didn't hurt anybody."

"How the hell are we going to kill her?"

"I don't know, but I'm not going to lose sleep over it. When the time comes, we'll figure something out. Goodnight, partner."

"Night, Mike. I'll see you in the morning."

Friday, December 17th, 2010

The Morning America news team aired footage of the situation that occurred on Wednesday. The video had been held back for a day as producers decided how much they could justify showing the public. Mike's shot to Sarah's head had been edited, for a number of reasons. But they showed the footage of him putting two bullets into Gloria Knecht's chest to absolutely no effect. Then Jackie came on camera, her eyes glazed and tear-filled after seeing the video again. It was difficult to remain professional and distant when viewing a tragedy, but she gave it her best shot.

"As you can see, bullets have absolutely no effect on the vampire, so all I can really say, for everyone watching, is pray like you have never prayed before. We can only hope that God will see fit to end this reign of terror." She stood up and walked off camera, something she had never done before in her career, and wept.

Brian Miller was stunned as he watched. He couldn't even imagine how Sara and Mike were feeling, not only at that terrifying moment, but today. The post-traumatic stress must be horrific. How the hell were they going to kill this thing?

****

Lasky also watched the video and reached into his desk drawer. He pulled out a bottle of Jim Beam, uncapped it, and took a long swallow right from the bottle. Only eight days to go until either the vampire claimed her last victim or good finally won out. He took Jackie up on her advice and got down on his knees and prayed harder and longer than he ever had in his life.

****

Jack arrived at the Bethlehem Steel Club shooting range and set up his pumpkins. He locked and loaded his rifle, which held four of the homemade rounds, and sighted in from seventy-five yards away. Then he took a breath and slowly squeezed the trigger.

The recoil wasn't bad, considering he hadn't fired a Savage before. The pumpkin exploded, and Jack quickly fired the other three rounds into the remaining pumpkins, sadly watching each one burst apart. The rounds went right through, so it was highly unlikely that this method would work.

He took out his cell and called Lasky.

****

Even after the workday concluded, and the lights of the city and the Star of Bethlehem glowed bright in the early darkness, the shoppers still came out in droves, in defiance of the danger. Who would ever be able to figure out human nature?

Even though the shopkeepers were on the alert, they still had to make a living. If people were going to come into their stores and spend money, whether to make themselves feel better or just acting out of habit, retail was a tough road to plow, and this time of year could either make them or break them, so they kept their stores open.

Restaurants were busier than ever. There were only eight shopping days left until Christmas, and shoppers were always hungry, so the restaurant owners, too, refused to shut down. Several of the eateries had hired off-duty cops to patrol their establishments. The cops wore street clothes and kept their weapons hidden, even though they knew bullets would not stop the vampire.

Tree branches were festooned with white lights. The famous Main Street lamps were covered with greens. Out on the street, a carriage was pulled by two white horses, guided by a man dressed in a tuxedo and wearing a top hat. The carriage carried a young family on a tour of that part of the city. Christmas carols could be heard emanating from many of the shops.

The early evening seemed so idyllic and relaxing that Gloria Knecht felt quite at east in the midst of the tourists. She felt safe, walking at night, imagining the many Christmases to come that would become the most wonderful times of her life. Although her face would be recognizable all over the world, she knew of several doctors who could create a new face for her, no questions asked. All it would take was lots of money. After one hundred and seventy five years on this earth, she had amassed a fortune in gold, silver, jewels and art. She could easily sell off some of it to get the extra funds. She also had several million dollars in cash, hidden in a number of locations across the United States. She smiled, nearly tasting the freedom that would be hers in just a few short days.

****

Roy Clayton was signing books at the Moravian Book Shop, thrilled by the response his work was receiving, both in the brick-and-mortar stores and online. He was racking up a considerable amount of money and had begun to seriously consider quitting his part-time job so that he could spend more time writing.

He'd been dismayed when he saw that bullets passed right through the vampire's body, but he had high hopes for the new suggestion he had offered to Lasky. He'd find out about its feasibility in the next day or two.

****

As the evening wore on, more and more people finished their shopping and satisfied their hunger. They were ready to go home and get a good night's sleep. The workday would come, all too soon.

Brian Miller and Jessie Sterling were cuddled up on his sofa, next to a roaring fireplace. They had spent the past several hours talking, as they ate snacks and watched TV. Around ten thirty, they rose, turned off the gas fireplace and the lights, and went to the bedroom.

After switching on the nightstand lamp, Jessie walked into the bathroom while Brian pulled down the shade at their back window.

He thought he saw a shadowy figure outside, standing by a tree, but as he looked harder, he realized that nothing was there. He peered out one more time, then shook his head, telling himself that his mind must just be playing tricks on him.

Saturday, December 18th, 2010

Even though his heart was still broken, Jim Blackman decided to reopen the shop. He knew that, once he stepped inside, he would probably break down again, seeing all the reminders of Jenna throughout the interior of the store. She'd had a real knack for decorating, and for displaying each item in just the right place to catch the shopper's eye. And she had been the same way at home, with each season represented throughout the house. He especially loved the way she decorated for the Christmas season, but the decorating came to an abrupt halt twenty-three days ago, with her murder. When he came back home that day, after finding out about her death, he'd looked over the numerous Clothtique and Pipka Santas, plus her growing collection of Byers Carolers, and stifled a sob. They would remain as they were until the beginning of next year, then be boxed up and, perhaps, never displayed again. He had a moment when he thought he would lose his composure, but held it together. He always thought himself to be a strong man, but losing Jenna was the toughest thing he ever faced.

Once he finished eating, he walked to the shop and cried when he saw the memorial of flowers, pictures, and wreaths that were piled from the front of the store to the street. A yellow-taped police barrier surrounded the makeshift memorial, forcing pedestrians to walk out into the street to get around it, and he was amazed that the police department would even allow such a large memorial. Touched at seeing pictures of Jenna with friends, he was able to push through the pain of her loss and recognize how much she had been loved.

When he had cleared a path and opened the store, he was caught unaware by the scents of the many different candles There was no longer any trace of Jenna's perfume, and that made it easier for him to be back in the shop.

After he and a couple of neighbor shopkeepers took all of the items from the pavement into the back room, he peeled off the Sorry We Missed You stickers from UPS, USPS and FedEx from the glass window of the door. Then he took up his position behind the cash register and heaved a deep sigh as he waited for the first shoppers.

Before long, before several customers had stepped in, selected items and left, only to be replaced by others.

He called a friend who had a pickup truck with a cap and asked if he could come to the store, deliver the notices to the three package-service deliverers, and pick up the orders, so that Jim could begin restocking. Soon, he found himself smiling, for the first time since Jenna's death, and realized that he would was going to be okay again. He would miss her every day until he died, but he would go on with his life.

****

Jack, along with several expert archers, had gathered in the hope of figuring out how to make glass arrowheads that could be loaded with holy water and still perform properly. The weight on the front of the shaft would create a number of problems, but they were hopeful that, after a series of tests, they'd come up with a way that arrows could fly true to their target.

Jack called a friend who blew glass at the Banana Factory and asked him to see what he and his co-workers could create. The glass had to be brittle enough to break on impact, but strong enough to carry a couple of ounces of holy water inside. Julie Christopher said she'd give it her best shot, but warned that it might take some time to design such an arrow point.

****

Brian Miller was working his butt off at the post office. The final Saturday before Christmas was always brutal; the number of packages he had to deliver filled the back of his truck, leaving a lot less room for his trays and tubs of mail. He knew it would be a long day, especially since he'd have to deviate from his route to deliver the fourteen large packages first so that he'd be able to get at his letters and flat mail.

He and Jessie had enjoyed a wonderful night, the previous night, just cuddling on the sofa, watching TV, eating snacks and drinking beer. They'd ended the evening making love until they were exhausted. He was still troubled by the thought that he saw someone outside his window, but he shrugged it off.

Jessie had to go to work this morning, too, because she had a ton of letters to type and a pile of mail to respond to. Her bosses were busy in court, with little time to indulge in the more relaxed atmosphere of the office.

Brian arranged to meet her for lunch around noon and she told him she was pretty sure that she'd have enough work under her belt by then that she could go home and rest until his day was over.

****

Mike and Sara were also hard at work, writing parking tickets left and right. Shoppers had a tendency to forget the time when they were busy parting with their money. One was fortunate enough to get back to his car just before the meter expired. Mike smiled at him and nodded. He was happy after having a long talk with Sara, who had decided to stick it out on the police force. She really did love her job. After yesterday, though, she was nervous about what could happen to her or any of her fellow officers on any given day.

****

Carl Anderson was still hard at work, filling in the timeline of Gloria Knecht. He knew a great deal about her already, but was continuing to research murders from the past hundred and fifty years, hoping to find the answer for her destruction.

He'd been receiving emails from Hyram, but the latest one, informing him that bullets passed right through her body with no effect, really got to him. He had already ruled out stakes, drowning and water, but hearing about the creation of an arrow tip filled with holy water revved his motors again. He had an idea and called Lasky immediately.

"Hi, Carl. How's it going?"

"Well, I've uncovered a lot of information about our friend, but as far as destroying her, that's a tough gig. Still, I like the arrow bit. My suggestion would be to load not just the tip with holy water, but the whole shaft. If the tip disintegrates on contact, the holy water might not do its job. But the shaft will continue into her body, so that might do the trick -- if, or course, holy water has any effect on her at all."

"That's a good idea. I'll call Jack as soon as you and I are done here. I do agree that holy water might not work, but what other choices do we have? To our knowledge, nothing has harmed her, the few times she was seen. That display yesterday still damn near makes me vomit."

"I can imagine, Hyram. How are Officers McGinnis and Jameison doing? That must have been tough on both of them."

"They're going to be okay, but I think they'll probably relive that shooting for a long time."

"Yeah, you're probably right. Look, I'm not going to hold you up. Time is short. Have they reconnoitered already to find the highest spot overlooking the city?"

"Yeah, we have that pretty much covered. Jack found two possible sites, and I told him about another place on South Mountain. It's called Mountaintop, owned by Lehigh University, and the view from there is magnificent."

"Well, cover all your bases. I'll talk to you again real soon. Take care, my friend."

"You, too, Carl."

****

Lasky called the Banana Factory.

"Banana Factory. This is Norm Green."

"Hello, Mr. Green. This is Detective Lasky of the Bethlehem PD. How are you today?"

"I'm fine, sir. And you?"

"Not too bad. I'm calling to see if anyone has been put to work trying to create the special glass arrowheads I requested."

"Yes, Detective. One of our best glassblowers, Julie Christopher, is working on that project at this very moment."

"Would it be possible to speak to her?"

"Certainly. I'll page her right now. Hang on for a moment, please."

****

Julie was diligently working on the creation of a hollow arrowhead. Several of her attempts had resulted in the glass simply melting because of its thinness, and she was becoming agitated over not being able to come up with a solution. When she heard her name being paged, she picked up a phone. "Julie Christopher here. May I help you?"

"Hi, Miss Christopher. This is Detective Lasky. I was calling to see how the arrowhead project is coming along."

"Detective, making one properly is giving me fits, but I'm sure I'll come up with a solution sometime soon. The tough thing is making the glass brittle enough to shatter on impact but strong enough to hold the water. I just need some more time."

"I appreciate everything you're doing, really, but our time is growing short and we need quite a few arrowheads for our archers to practice with, in order to make this work. A friend passed on the idea that filling the arrow shaft with holy water, too, would increase the archers' chances."

"I can do that, Detective. As Scotty would say to Kirk, 'I'll give it all I got, Captain.'"

Lasky laughed out loud. "Thanks, Julie. I needed that. Get back to me soon."

"I will, Detective."

Sunday, December 19th, 2010

Churches all around the country were once again packed with congregation members and visitors. Collection plates overflowed, which would put many of the religious institutions in the black for the first time that year.

Mike and Jean attended the first traditional service of the day, then drove to town for breakfast, listening to an oldies station, both lost in their own thoughts.

Surprisingly, after arriving at Billy's Downtown Diner, they were escorted to a table after only a five minute wait. Their food was served in a short time as well. As they ate their meal, Jean put her hand on top of Mike's, causing him to stop and focus his full attention on her.

"Mike, I've been thinking an awful lot about us, about you and your job, and especially about how you saved Sara's life on Friday. You are a great cop."

"Thanks. I really didn't want to shoot that woman, but I felt I had no other choice."

"I know. But chances are, there will be other times like that…and one time you might not make it home." She looked down at her plate for a moment, and when she looked up at him again, her eyes were filled with tears. "I know you'll never give up being a cop. You love it too much. But I'm on edge, every day you're out there."

"Jean, I…"

She placed a finger to his lips, silencing him. "I can't go on like this any longer, Mike. I don't want to wind up the widow of a cop. While we were at church, I had my sister go to the house and pack a couple of bags for me. I have to get out of here before I go crazy. I've already contacted an attorney, and I'm going to file for divorce."

Mike dropped his fork, the noise diverting nearby diners' stares to their table. "Are you sure you want to do this before talking it over some more?"

She took his hand again and nodded. "You know how that conversation would wind up, Mike. I will always love you, but I just can't stay with you anymore." She stood up, grabbed her coat and burst through the crowd waiting for seats and into her sister's car.

Mike got up from the table, paid the tab and drove home to a house that held memories, good and bad.

****

Sara awakened early and decided to go running. She drove her car to the Murray Goodman Campus of Lehigh University and took off on a path used by many Lehigh athletes, students, and local residents

The morning air was crisp and refreshing as she stretched for a few minutes before beginning her run. Then she started slowly, gradually picking up speed as she began passing by homes to her right. She noticed a man, clad in baggy jeans, a flannel shirt and a sweatshirt, standing on his deck, a cup of coffee in one hand and a book in the other. Sara smiled when she recognized him as a lawyer she had spoken to a couple of times. She waved, and the man lifted his cup in greeting as she ran past and turned left.

The path wound its way through trees on both sides and a creek on the right. Her eyes moved constantly, scanning left to right, since there were numerous places for a possible attacker to hide. Gloria Knecht could be anywhere, but Sara took comfort from the thought of the gun in her ankle holster.

Suddenly, she detected movement to her left. Turning to look, she saw a seven-point buck scamper through the hilly wooded area. The magnificent animal leapt over a fallen tree and broke through the wood line into a harvested corn field, where he took off like the proverbial bat out of hell.

Sara broke out into the open, running up a slight grade until she was on the other side of the wooded area. Looking back, she saw a runner coming up the path she had just taken. Even though the two of them were only a few yards apart at that point, Sara was a good quarter of a mile ahead. By the time she reached the halfway point of her run, however, the other runner caught up and passed her with ease. As she ran by, Sara admired the woman's strong, bare legs…until she recognized a familiar tattoo on her calf.

Sara stopped in mid-stride and went down on her left knee, pulling up the bottom of her jogging pants and grabbing the gun in one quick motion. She quickly fired three rounds, each one passing through the runner's body with no effect. The shots startled the hell out of a trio of walkers and their three dogs. She heard the younger of the two women, who held a black dog on a leash, scream, and she saw the man reach out for her. The dogs began to bark and snarl.

Gloria Knecht ran past the threesome and their pets, flipping Sara the finger and smiling wickedly. She turned and ran at an unbelievable speed until she rounded the corner of the wood line to her right and was out of sight.

Sara raced to see if the people and their animals were okay.

The woman who had screamed nodded, but said, "I know who that was. I saw her fangs." She started to shake from the adrenaline rush.

****

Later on that afternoon, Mike was sulking in his living room, drinking beer. He knew leaving was the best thing for her. Someday, as she'd said, his luck would run out and she would become a widow. Now, instead, she'd be able to find a man who didn't run around with a gun strapped to his hip, sometimes looking for trouble instead of letting trouble find him.

He shuffled out to the kitchen for his fourth or fifth beer; he couldn't quite remember which it was, and that didn't bode well, because he was surely getting drunk.

His cell phone rang and he answered.

"Mike, I've been trying to reach you for hours. Are you okay?"

"Yeah, Shara," he slurred. "I turned off my phone before church and just remembered to turn it back on a couple of beers ago." He took a deep breath, trying to clear his head. "I have something to tell you."

"Really? That makes two of us who have something to talk about."

"Okay, you go first."

She heard a pop tab being pulled, and wondered what was making him drink so much. "This morning, I was out for a run. About halfway through the course, a woman in shorts passed me. I saw the half-moon tattoo on her calf and I fired three rounds, but I failed to hit her. I knew the bullets wouldn't have any effect on her, and I shouldn't have fired. Three people and their dogs were nearly in my line of fire. She's really getting to me, partner."

Mike sat down hard in a kitchen chair. "Gloria was stalking you again? Did anybody get hurt? Are you okay?"

"No one got hurt, but one of the women saw Gloria's fangs and she was quite upset but I stayed with her until she calmed down. Gloria didn't try anything with me. I think she just wanted to show off her speed and toss a little of her sick vampire humor at me. She bared her fangs and flipped me the bird."

Mike had to laugh in spite of the gravity of what she was saying. "Shorry, Shara, it's just the way you said that that made me laugh. You always have a way of making me laugh when I'm having problems."

"So what's up with you? You sound like you've been drinking pretty heavily."

He nodded his head, then realized she wouldn't be able to see that motion. "I've had maybe four or five beers in a couple of hours, and I'm a little trashed. Too much shit going on."

"So what else is going on?"

"Jean left me, Sar."

"Oh, Mike! I'm so sorry. I know you were trying to fix things."

"It's the job, partner. She doesn't want to become a widow, although I suppose that could still happen before the ink dries on the divorce decree. Hell, I could be dead before Christmas, and then she'd definitely be a widow." He chuckled. "Well, that way, I guess she'd get everything without having to give some lawyer a huge piece of change for handling the paperwork."

"Would you like me to come over, so we can talk in person?"

Mike hesitated, wondering if it would be a good idea to start something with his gay partner, especially since he was still married. But that was his head talking. He knew what he wanted. "Yes, Sara. I'd love it if we could talk."

"Great. I'll pick up a pizza on the way. See you later."

****

Shortly after darkness fell, Jim Humanick, a member of the Lehigh Valley Amateur Astronomical Society, was observing the night sky when he came upon something startling. As he continued to watch, he took measurements and then fed the numbers into a computer.

"This is impossible," he said aloud when he saw the results, even though no one else was in the building. He entered the information, but the same answer appeared on the screen. He called the University of Pennsylvania Observatory, hoping someone would be there.

After seven or eight rings, someone picked up. "Hello? University of Pennsylvania Observatory, Chad Mellinger speaking. How may I help you?"

"Hi, Mr. Mellinger. This is Jim Humanick of the Lehigh Valley Amateur Astronomical Society. I just made a discovery that seems quite impossible, and I was hoping you might be able to take a look."

"Sure. What are you seeing?"

"I've been viewing and taking measurements of Jupiter and Venus, and my conclusion is that they are closing together and will align horizontally on Christmas Eve."

"Well, Jim, that doesn't sound feasible…but let me write down your number and I'll get back to you, after I take a look."

Jim had paid close attention to the tone of his voice. "Mr. Mellinger, I'm not crazy, if that's what you're thinking. What's happening out there is real."

"Okay, Jim. I'll take a look and get back to you soon."

"Thanks."

****

Chad sat down, placed his eye to the scope and began to search. When he saw the two planets, and how close their proximity was, he became a believer. Feeding numbers into a computer. He came to the same conclusion. Venus and Jupiter were converging and would align on Christmas Eve. This alignment would generate a light brighter than anything ever seen at night.

After he called Jim back to verify his figures, he elicited help from a friend in the science department, to see when this astronomical anomaly would occur.

Later that evening, his friend returned the call. "Chad, with all the figures you gave me, I conclude that the planets will be in alignment around six PM on Christmas Eve, and I think they'll stay in alignment for quite some time, perhaps an hour. It looks like we're going to see a Christmas star only seen once before in the history of the world."

"The star that guided all those people to Bethlehem to see the baby Jesus?"

"The same kind of star, Chad. You're right. And to top it off, it will be at its brightest as it hovers over Bethlehem, Pennsylvania. Quite a coincidence, wouldn't you agree?"

"Yeah, but I believe that celestial event is supposed to happen here for a reason. Maybe God is going to pitch in to help destroy a vampire."

"I sure hope so, Chad. I know the killings have all been in Bethlehem, but what if she decides to move on? People won't be safe anywhere and the sheer terror of that possibility could drive large numbers of people to the brink of despair."

"That's possibly true. Let's just hope that, with God's help, the vampire will no longer exist after Christmas Eve."

"Take care, Chad. And may you and yours have a wonderful Christmas and a Happy New Year."

"You, too. Thanks for your help."

After the conversation ended, he called Jim to inform him, then he went back to the telescope, determined to keep watch over the converging planets.

Monday, December 20th, 2010

Mike awakened and strolled out to the kitchen to make coffee and breakfast, feeling better than he had in months. Upon Sara's arrival, the previous night, he hadn't really known how everything would go, but after he opened the door and saw her carrying an overnight bag and her uniform, there was no doubt in his mind that she was ready to try to make love with a man again. After a great deal of time spent talking, weighing the pros and cons of beginning a relationship before he was divorced, they both agreed that Jean would never reconsider her decision. They went to bed, slowly undressing each other, kissing and hugging for a long time before making love slowly, as Sara reacquainted herself with heterosexual sex.

A few minutes later, she came into the kitchen, smelling the coffee. Sara tiptoed up to Mike and gave him a hug. He turned and they kissed. She wasn't wearing a stitch, and they sank to the floor and made love again as the coffee perked on the counter beside them.

While Sara enjoyed a cup of coffee, Mike fried up six eggs and several slices of Spam, then put four slices of bread into the toaster. After they hurriedly ate, they raced to the shower, washing each other quickly, knowing that they would have to get a move on, to make it to roll call on time.

****

Julie Christopher got an early start on the day, hoping finally to be able to make the glass arrowheads perfectly. She was increasingly afraid, because she would be in the middle of her menstrual cycle on Christmas Eve, and she didn't want to become a statistic. Several times over the past few days, she had felt that she was being shadowed, but whenever she looked around, no one seemed to be paying any particular attention to her. Julie was ready to blame her fears on an overactive imagination, but not to the point where she became careless.

She strode to the furnace and gathered some glass on the end of her blowpipe. Inserting the hot glass into an arrowhead-shaped mold she had created, Julie slowly blew into her pipe and then covered the hole so the trapped air could work its way into the glass. She watched the molten glass take its shape and then she pulled it out from the mold. She took a 'jack' – stylized long tongs – to break the arrowhead off the pipe.

Once the glass cooled, Julie ground the open end of the arrowhead smooth and placed it carefully in a vise and inserted the arrowhead. Next, she removed one of the fifty aluminum arrow shafts that Jack had dropped off, and filled it with water. She then inserted the shaft into the opening of the arrowhead.

After heating the base of the arrowhead, and allowing it to cool, she removed the assembled arrow from the vise and pointed the tip in a downward angle. The water flowed into it freely, and she smiled. She had accomplished her mission. Now, all she had to do was to make forty-nine more.

It was going to be a long day.

****

Brian Miller was tired. He and Jessie had enjoyed a wonderful day, but the woman was insatiable. Not that he was complaining, but his back was a little sore, and today would be the heaviest delivery day of the year.

When he walked to his case and saw three trays of letter mail, mainly Christmas cards, but only one tub of flats, he was not too unhappy. A lot depended on how much DPS mail there would be. Before going back to the punch clock, he looked to see if the DPS report was on the supervisor's desk, but it wasn't. He saw several clerks tossing parcels into the orange hampers, and noticed that his was filled to the brim. He shook his head, knowing it would be another long day.

At the punch clock, he bullshitted with a few of the guys as they waited for the clock to tick to their assigned starting time. After clocking in, they all walked out to the parking lot to check their trucks, the smokers lighting up because they wouldn't have time for another until they headed out to the street.

****

Hyram Lasky hung up the phone after his brief conversation with Julie, then immediately called Jack to tell him that the arrows were ready.

"That's great. Thanks." Jack then called the three archers he'd found to be available for the week and asked them to meet him at the range where they would each test fire six arrows. That would still leave over two dozen for the actual event, and Jack was sure that they would never get the opportunity to launch more than a couple of arrows apiece toward Gloria Knecht. They had to kill her while she was still a vampire, before she took the life of one more woman. If that were to happen, the assignment was to capture her so she could stand trial for all the murders she'd committed, although he figured that the courts would have their hands full trying to find enough evidence to make the older deaths provable.

As Jack drove to the Banana Factory to pick up the arrows, the thought crossed his mind that Gloria would never become human again, and if she succeeded in killing her 'final' victim, she could remain a vampire forever. Perhaps the witch only told her that she would become a human again to torment her. How would Gloria react if she completed her one-hundred-and-fifty-year curse and then became a vampire forever? Jack was afraid that, if that happened, she would go on a killing spree for a long time to come.

He gripped the steering wheel harder. He and his team had to succeed. They simply had to.

Later, at the range, the four archers tested the arrows and found they worked perfectly. The video cameras that were set up caught all the hits. When the team reviewed the footage in slow motion, they saw the arrows penetrate the target, breaking apart upon entry. When they inspected the targets, they found that all of the holy water had been released, just the way they had hoped. The only question left was whether the arrowheads would break after entering Gloria's body, or would simply pass through, like the bullets did. There were way too many ifs in the equation, and Jack was beginning to believe that some divine intervention would have to occur to destroy the vampire.

****

Gloria Knecht spent most of the day in her motel room, waiting for nightfall before venturing out, not wanting anyone to recognize her, this close to the end.

At six AM, she turned on the television to see what the stars of Morning America had to say today. The night she broke the TV in her room, she found a vacant room, and after some effort, was able to jimmy the door open. She carried the TV from there back to hers, removing the broken one and getting rid of it before housekeeping had an opportunity to see the mess when they came in to clean her room.

Since there wasn't any new vampire news, the news team had gone back to their normal routine of talking about politics. Gloria quickly grew tired of the banter and found an old movie to watch – although, of course, to her it wasn't an 'old' movie, since she had seen it when it first came to the theaters in 1947.

When the sun finally set, she was ready to end her cabin fever and get back out into the world of humanity again. Main Street would probably be packed with people concluding their shopping and having dinner or drinks. She was tempted to stop by the Brew Works for a drink. But she resisted. It would be just too risky.

****

Mike and Sara ended their workday after talking for hours while they patrolled.

Sara was much more comfortable with him now, but her guts were still churning. She wanted to be with him all the time, but she couldn't be sure she wouldn't get the urge to be with women again at some point down the road. She sighed audibly, causing Mike to turn toward her. Sara smiled at him and touched his leg, assuring him that nothing was wrong.

They worked together in the kitchen creating a wonderful meal, watched a little TV, and took a shower together, having sex as the hot water cascaded down their bodies. After toweling off, they climbed into bed, exhausted.

Sleep came quickly, but Sara woke up in the middle of the night after another horrendous nightmare. She clenched her fists, knowing that if Gloria Knecht wasn't killed on Christmas Eve, she might not live to see Christmas Day.

It was only after an hour of tossing and turning that she finally went back to sleep.

Tuesday, December 21st, 2010

Gloria Knecht awakened with a splitting headache.

She couldn't recall ever having had one, in the entire period of time she had been forced to take human blood to keep herself alive for another decade. She sat up and stared at the red numbers on the digital clock on the nightstand, and saw that the time was two forty-one AM. She then remembered hearing about the total lunar eclipse that was to coincide with the winter solstice. On that particular newscast, she also heard that that last full eclipse of the moon during the winter solstice had occurred in 1638.

She threw on a robe and stepped out onto the balcony to view the rare event.

As the earth's shadow completely covered the moon's surface, her head felt as if it was going to explode. Off in the distance, she heard the howls of what sounded like wolves, but she knew that there were no wolves in Pennsylvania. Perhaps they were dogs baying at the eclipse… But no. She was that certain the sound was wolves, having heard and seen them when she was a young girl, all those years ago.

As she watched the eclipse unfold, she saw the moon become a ball of orange, caused by some of the sun's rays hitting its surface. At that moment, the pain became unbearable. She pressed her hands to her head and squeezed as hard as she could, hoping to ease the pain with the pressure she created, but it didn't help at all. She writhed in agony, falling to her knees, wondering if this was the way she was going to die. It terrified her that this event might end her existence before she had the opportunity to regain her humanity and live out a normal life.

Gloria struggled to regain her feet and wobbled back inside her room, collapsing on the bed, tears streaming down her face, her body convulsing involuntarily. But just when she thought she couldn't take anymore, her headache subsided, as quickly as it had begun. She breathed deeply and went back out onto the balcony to see the moon coming out from the earth's shadow. She let out a great sigh of relief and then went back to bed, feeling much better, but weak in the knees.

****

At one thirty AM, Brian Miller's alarm clock beeped.

He quickly shut it off, not wanting to awaken Jessie. Jumping out of bed, he threw on some warm clothes and ventured outside to see the total eclipse of the moon. He knew he was going to pay for it at work, later that day, but he wanted to witness the event firsthand, and not have one of his buddies tease him about being a wimp and sleeping through the rare occurrence.

Brian walked through the community until he found a vantage point where he could witness the eclipse from beginning to end. It was due to last nearly two and a half hours, and he hoped that when he crawled back into bed, he'd fall asleep right away and at least get a couple more hours of rest before reporting to the post office.

Soon after he sat down on the grass, he was joined by another idiot. This one had brought a camcorder and was going to record the entire event. Brian had settled for setting his DVR on one of the news channels that would show the full coverage of the winter solstice eclipse, figuring that he would watch it sometime in the future. But seeing the event as it happened was a pretty cool thing to do.

As he waited for the eclipse to begin, he struck up a conversation with the man. "I know I'm a little crazy, sitting out here on snow-covered grass to see the eclipse, but what about you?" He stuck out his hand. "I'm Brian Miller."

The man laughed and took his hand, shaking it vigorously. ""I'm Ben Fritz. I've been having trouble sleeping lately, since I dislocated my hip. I figured, what the hell, why not make some use of my time?"

Brian nodded his head. "I know you. You're a retired Marine. You hang out with that author, Roy Clayton."

"Yeah, we're friends. I didn't think I'd like his vampire book but, with all this shit going down, I figured I ought to get a copy and read it. I saw him on Saturday morning and sat down as soon as I got home. I read it in one sitting and I thought it was pretty good, for a first-time author." He pulled a flask from his fatigue jacket and lifted it to his lips. After taking a few swallows, he turned to Brian. "Care for a snort?"

Brian took the flask and had a taste. "Good shit, Ben, but I better not drink too much. I gotta be at work at seven." He handed it back.

"You can handle it, man. You're young and healthy."

Not knowing what else to talk about, they sat quietly for a while. The silence was broken by howling just as the eclipse began. Ben put his camcorder to work, but they glanced at each other in surprise at the sound. "Wolves?"

At four AM, Brian was back in his bed, and asleep in minutes.

****

At six AM, the Morning America team was seated in their chairs outside the Bethlehem Public Library. The total eclipse was being shown on a large video screen at a fast speed, allowing viewers to watch the event in minutes instead of hours.

Despite her makeup, Jackie looked extremely tired; she had watched the eclipse live and then had several cups of coffee before dressing and arriving at the outdoor studio at five.

Although the planned destruction of Gloria Knecht was on everyone's mind, there was little new to report, so the crew decided to do something a little different. They selected several members of the audience to join them in a discussion about what Christmas meant to them.

One of the impromptu guests caught everyone by surprise when she said that this would be her last Christmas on earth.

"A few days ago, I received the news that I only have a few more months to live. I have a rare type of ovarian cancer. I'm glad I've had the opportunity to sit with you folks, this morning, because most of us never get the chance to know how long we have left on this earth. As a Christian woman, I'd just like to say that the Christmas season means so much to me because our Lord Jesus's birthday is celebrated on December 25th. Too many of us have forgotten what Christmas really means, but I've never forgotten. I wish I could live to celebrate many more of His birthdays, but soon I'll be with Him, and I don't want anyone to feel sorry for me. My

Christmas wish for all Morning America viewers is to really remember what Christmas is all about. Give for the spirit of making people happy, not hoping to receive something in return. If you don't belong to a church, or rarely go, please renew your faith." With tears streaming down her face, she left the stage, and the silence that followed for a lengthy moment spoke volumes.

****

Immediately after the woman left the outdoor studio, the video clip went viral, attracting millions of views over the course of the day. Salvation Army pots were filled to overflowing. Non-profit organizations reported hundreds of donations in the Lehigh Valley alone. The woman's message was broadcast on all the news networks, as well as the Internet, and people began using their cell phones to make pledges. Though a final tally of donations would not be possible for a long time to come, reports claimed that many millions of dollars were flooding in to hospitals, homeless shelters, the Red Cross, and churches around the world.

Shoppers began to think more carefully about their purchases, selecting gifts that would be more meaningful to the recipients than those they had originally planned to buy.

Wednesday, December 22nd, 2010

Jim Blackman was enjoying breakfast at Billy's, thinking about Jenna and how much he missed her. He had tried to return his life to as much normalcy as possible, but the void in his heart was a constant reminder of his loneliness.

The previous night, as he sorted though some things in his closet, he had found a small, beautifully wrapped gift, stashed behind several boxes of shoes. Carrying it to the bed, he'd read the inscription on the little tag: "To the love of my life. Love Jenna." Sitting down hard, Jim untied the bow, stripped the wrapping paper from the box and opened the lid.

He stared at the watch inside for a long time before removing it and reading the inscription on the back: *Always and Forever - Jenna.* Jim placed the watch on his left wrist. He had loved that watch, every time he saw it in the store, but it was expensive and he hadn't wanted to pay the price. Now it seemed that Jenna had squirreled away money and bought it for him for Christmas.

He thought about the half-dozen gifts he had hidden around the house, gifts that she would now never experience the joy of wearing.

He finished his breakfast and looked up as the restaurant owner, Billy Kounoupis, approached. "How are you doing, my friend?" Billy inquired as he picked up Jim's check.

"I'm getting better, Billy, but I miss her so much." He held out his wrist, displaying the watch. "I found this in a box in my closet, last night. After I put it on, I really broke down."

Billy looked at the watch. "I know it's hard, losing someone." He placed his hand on Jim's shoulder for a moment, then handed the twenty back. "Merry Christmas, Jim. Breakfast is on me."

Jim nodded his thanks and left the restaurant. On the way to the store, he saw Marilyn McGee walking toward him. A cameraman was beside her, and she stopped to sign a couple of autographs. She walked past him, flashing her great smile, then opened the door and stepped inside Billy's as the man lifted the camera to his shoulder.

****

Sara and Mike were cruising west on Broad Street when they saw Marilyn entering the front door of Billy's Downtown Diner with the cameraman. Sara found a parking spot a few blocks away, her curiosity piqued. They needed to know what was going on…and besides, coffee sounded really good to her, right then.

****

Brian Miller called in sick; he badly needed a 'mental health' day. He could only remember one other time in his career that he played hooky was to play golf a few years ago. Today, however, was different. He and Jess, who had the day off from the law firm, needed to do some serious Christmas shopping outside the city.

Both of them had already made numerous purchases from stores in downtown Bethlehem, but they hadn't found everything they wanted to get for each other. But Brian knew a great place in Lititz that sold estate jewelry. He hoped that Jess would see something she would fall in love with but wouldn't buy for herself. In addition, after thinking about what the woman on Morning America had said, they decided to make several purchases to donate to the church for the homeless.

After an early breakfast at the Hellertown Diner, they hopped into Jessie's car. Brian's 'piece of shit' Toyota had finally died, so they would have to make do with one car until Brian could find a suitable replacement, after Gloria was killed or captured.

Bellies full, the two of them began the drive to their first destination: Lititz, Pennsylvania.

****

When Roy Clayton had received word from Hyram that the arrows had passed the test, he was so elated that he started a lengthy conversation with Riley.

The dog placed his front paws on Roy's thighs and listened intently, cocking his head with each change of inflection in his man-friend's voice. Occasionally, Riley responded by licking Roy on his goatee and cheeks.

Susan Clayton, dressed for work, heard her husband talking and stopped short of the living room, not wanting to intrude on the bond that the man and animal shared. After their one-sided conversation came to an end, she stepped into the living room. "Honey that is such great news."

Man and dog looked her way, and Riley bounded over to leap up and down, eager for the piece of rawhide in her outstretched hand. After three leaps, he succeeded in snatching the treat from her hand, then scampered under the dining room table to enjoy it.

Sue laughed and shook her head. "Roy, it never ceases to amaze me how you can keep Riley's attention like you do."

Roy held out his hands, palms up, raising them toward the ceiling. "It's a gift, you know."

She came to him and leaned over. "You are so full of crap, my husband." She kissed him on the lips, then started toward the door.

"Honeybunny, keep your fingers crossed. The agent I hired might call today about a deal he's working on. If everything goes well, you'll be able to quit working and we'll be able to buy that home we like in Duck."

"It would be nice, being retired and able to go to our house on the Outer Banks anytime we wanted to. I'll be praying for us. Call me as soon as you find out."

"I will. See you later."

After she drove away, Roy looked at Riley, who was still busily chewing the rawhide. "Come on, Ri. Time to get busy on the computer. We need to write three thousand words today."

****

Hyram Lasky was sitting at his desk, going through the heavy volume of mail that had been piling up. Since the morning had brought no new Gloria Knecht reports, it seemed like an opportune time to catch up.

He was reading a letter from an irate citizen complaining about the lack of parking near her house because of all the additional people coming into town, when the phone rang. He picked up, glad of an excuse to put down the letter. "Bethlehem P D, Detective Lasky speaking."

"Hy. Carl Anderson."

Lasky gripped the edge of his desk in anticipation. "Carl! What can I do for you?"

"I've been thinking about a way to find Gloria before Christmas Eve. I was watching a movie, the other night, and I saw how some cops were after a killer. The killer had used a lot of aliases in his lifetime of crime, and the cops queried all the local hotels to see if anyone was registered under any of those names. So I printed a list of all the names we know about that Gloria has used in the past hundred and fifty years. I've taken the liberty of adding possible male names to the surnames, and I'm going to fax that list to you now."

"Great, Carl. As soon as I get the list, I'll fax it to all the local police stations so they can check out the lodgings in their sectors. I don't know if it will work, but anything is worth a shot, to try to get her before Christmas Eve."

As he was speaking, a secretary brought him the fax.

"Carl, I have it." He shook his head. "It's a sizable list. Thanks."

"You're welcome, Hy. I wish I could do more, but I can't think of anything else to do."

"My friend, you've done enough. Someday I'd sure like to meet you face to face."

"That would be splendid. We'll talk again after this business is over. Take care."

Eager to get started, Lasky broke the connection and waved a secretary over. "Here. Would you please get this list faxed to every PD in the Lehigh Valley?" he asked, writing as he spoke. "And here's a cover note, explaining what I want every available police officer to do, once they have this list."

****

When Sara and Mike walked into Billy's, Marilyn was standing at the counter chatting with Billy while the cameraman was setting up. The cops squeezed by him, and they parked themselves in a booth, ordering coffee and one order of Billy's famous Chocolatey Chip Pancakes. Both of them were engrossed in watching the interview preparations and ten minutes passed by before both Marilyn and the cameraman were ready for the interview. Finally she was ready to speak with Mike and Sara eager to listen in.

"Hello everyone. I'm at one of the Lehigh Valley's best eateries, Billy's Downtown Diner on Broad Street in Bethlehem" She turned toward Billy. "This is Billy Konnoupis. How long have you had your restaurant?"

"Well, Marilyn, I'm proud to say we opened in 2001, and we've served many, many people over the years."

"You've won some awards for serving the best breakfast in the Lehigh Valley…"

Mike and Sara's pancake arrived, so their attention was diverted back to their stomachs.

As Sara loaded a forkful of pancake and whipped cream, Mike looked at her. "Are you happy, honey?"

She smiled, nodded her head and filled her mouth with the decadent pancake. After she swallowed and wiped her mouth, she said, "Oh my God, Mike. That is so good. Can't have too many of these."

"No, you can't," he answered through a mouthful. His cell phone rang. "McGinnis." After listening a minute, he closed the phone. "Sara, we gotta eat fast. We have work to do. If things work out right, we may find Gloria today."

They finished their pancake and hurriedly drank their coffee. On the way out, Mike handed the cashier a twenty. "Keep the change."

When the two cops quickly exited the restaurant, many heads, including Marilyn's and Billy's, turned toward them.

Once in the car, Sara toggled the lights and siren and they did a quick U-turn and headed toward the Hotel Bethlehem.

****

Having finally caught up with all his correspondence, Hyram Lasky decided to take a much needed break.

Brushing snow off a nearby bench, he sat down, lit a cigarette and took a sip of hot coffee. The stress was beginning to wear on him. He wasn't sure if Carl Anderson's idea would work, but they had reached a point where there might not be much that anyone could do to find the vampire before she killed her final victim. He coughed up a wad of phlegm, vowing that as soon as Gloria was killed or captured he would try for the hundredth time to quit smoking and give up the hard stuff. Beer would be his alcohol of choice.

As he crushed the cigarette with his foot, his cell phone rang. "Lasky."

"Detective, this is Susan. We may have found Gloria Knecht. Please come to my desk."

Lasky was on his feet, running back to the office. "What do you have?"

"Officers Rhoades and Bachman are at the Comfort Inn on Highland Avenue." She handed him the phone.

"This is Detective Lasky. What do you have for me?"

"Detective, this is Tom Rhoades. We're at the Comfort Inn. When we checked the guest register, we found a listing for a guest named Adam Gibbs. It might be a stretch but, with all the derivations on the list, it's possible Gloria Knecht may have used that name as a substitute for Amelia Gibbons. I also checked back with the office, to see if anything concerning this place had been reported in the last couple of weeks."

"So, what did you find out?" Lasky asked with cautious excitement, hoping this might be the lead they needed.

"Well, sir, on Tuesday, the fourteenth, a car was reported stolen from the parking lot here. It was discovered two days later on Main Street, with a couple of parking tickets under the windshield wiper."

"Okay, Tom that does sound like a good possibility, but it's possible she's seen your patrol car in the lot. She may be ready for you guys to try to take her. And remember, bullets won't do shit to her. You guys should leave the premises and find a place where you can watch without being seen, until I figure out a plan."

"Yes, sir. I'm sure we can find a vantage point. I'll let you know when we're in place."

"Good job, Tom."

Lasky called Jack and asked him to send the archers over to the Comfort Inn and find some good cover to keep an eye on the place. "Maybe we can get her before she knows we're there. I'm gonna send a few detectives over, posing as tourists, to see if they can spot her and identify her before we go off half-cocked."

"No problem, Hyram. Me and my guys know how to pull off a sneaky Pete. If there's cover, we'll find it."

****

An hour later, Jack and three archers found positions where they could lay in wait, although none of them were sure how much they'd be able to see, once darkness fell. If no one could get a clean shot with the available light, Gloria would have a reprieve until daylight returned.

****

Gloria spotted one of the men. Standing at the window of her room, she glanced outside and saw the man duck behind a tree and pull out a bow from the case he was carrying. She saw him lay out several arrows and wondered what the hell he thought he could do with that. Bullets passed through her body; wooden stakes did the same. So how in the hell was someone going to bring her down with an arrow?

Though amused, she was also determined to take no chances, so close to the end of her journey. Once nightfall came, she would get her ass out of there and look for another place to stay until Friday.

To amuse herself for a couple of hours she sat down to read Roy Clayton's vampire novel.

****

As the sun went down and darkness covered the land, the archers agreed that there would be no way to get her, that night. Earlier they had all agreed that if she didn't present herself as a target, they would gather at the BBW for a couple of drinks and a strategy session. They decided to head out, and come back again before first light.

Later, after it was too dark to see, the archers packed up their gear and drove into town.

Thursday, December 23rd, 2010

Awakened from a deep sleep by the ringing of his phone, Jack McGinnis picked it up. "Hello?" he said groggily.

"Jack, it's Hyram. Sorry to wake you so early but you guys don't have to go to the Comfort Inn this morning. Gloria bailed, during the night."

Jack sat up so quickly that his head throbbed. "She bailed? Do you think she spotted one of us yesterday?"

"That's the conclusion I've come to, but with her, who the hell knows? Unless we find out where she's gone, we're back where we were on Tuesday. I guess I should have sent a team in with weapons, hoping to slow her down somehow, but I really didn't want to get any cops killed."

"You were right not to send anyone in. I'll call my guys and tell them to stay in bed. We all had a little too much to drink, last night, and I'll definitely need them fresh for tomorrow night."

"What's the big idea, getting trashed, last night? What if you guys had gotten a shot at her, this morning? I'm a little pissed, Jack."

"Yeah, I can see where you would be, but I figured we wouldn't get a chance at her until near sundown. We scrubbed our plan to come out before daylight, but I was going to head over there this morning to see if we could take her down inside the building somewhere. Guess I don't have to do that, either."

Hyram thought it over for a moment. "You could be right, but I just think you guys shouldn't drink till this is over. I can't tell you what to do, but consider this a strong suggestion."

"Okay, don't worry. When the time comes, we will be ready."

"Okay, get back to sleep if you can. If I hear anything, I'll give you a buzz."

"Thanks, Hy." He hung up the phone and was asleep again in minutes.

****

Brian Miller had taken a rasher of shit from his boss about being sick the day before, but he played the game to the hilt. "I still didn't feel too great this morning, boss. I was going to call in sick again, but I know how shorthanded we are, so I decided to come in."

His boss bought it, but now Brian was going to pay, because whoever had subbed for him had done as little as possible, and there was mail out the ying yang.

When he and Jessie had walked through the jewelry store, she'd shown real interest in a black diamond ring. One look told him he should buy it soon and put it away for the proper time. Although they had been lovers for such a short time, all the time he'd spent with her before, while delivering the mail, had left him convinced that he wanted to marry her, once all this vampire crap was behind them.

After they left the jewelry shop, Jessie told Brian that she had one more errand to run, and he had told her he was going to the bookshop. They parted company but, as soon as Jessie turned in at another storefront, Brian turned and headed back to the jewelry store.

He was able to make a deal quickly and stuff the ring into his pocket. Since Jess had already tried it on to admire it, he knew that it fit perfectly; he wouldn't have to get the engagement ring sized.

He was so happy with Jessie, and now she would have the perfect ring.

****

Morning America was broadcasting live from the Bethlehem Library. Their guests included all of the vampire novelists they had rounded up, along with several experts in the field of vampire lore. Since Gloria had remained out of sight, but not out of mind, they needed these guests to fill their three hours of air time. Some political talk was offered, as well, but it wasn't a good day in that arena since so many congressmen and senators were beginning their extended Christmas holiday.

****

Shoppers crowded Main Street, and the local malls were seeing a real upturn in business. At this rate, their year would end up in the black.

Jim Blackman was making a great deal of money, but his heart was aching. He missed Jenna more and more, but he knew she would want him to carry on.

****

After checking in at the Hotel Bethlehem disguised as a sixty-something woman of means, Gloria Knecht opened the curtains and peered out over the bustling crowds on Main Street. In less than thirty-six hours, she would once again be human. She pressed her face to the window, daydreaming of all the things she would be able to do and the places she would be able to go, with a new face and a whole new identity. The wait was driving her crazy, but wait she must. Seconds felt like minutes, and minutes like days, but soon the waiting would be over. Her final victim had been selected and she knew exactly when to strike.

When the moon was high in the sky and most everyone was in bed, she stretched out on hers, determined that her last night's sleep as a vampire would be a good one.

Friday, December 24th, 2010 Christmas Eve

In the final minutes before dawn, Lasky lit a cigarette and stepped outside his house to see if the paper had come early.

The paper wasn't there but, as he smoked, he happened to glance up at the sky, where he beheld a sight he had never seen before. Two stars appeared to be close together, and it was eye-catching. He hoped he'd be able to get a better look at it that night, but the odds were against him; it was supposed to be cloudy, with a forty percent chance of snow. Besides, there would be a lot of activity in the night ahead, if Gloria Knecht was found and boxed in somewhere. As he pondered the likelihood that they would be able to take her down with a bow and arrow, the knot began to reform in his stomach, and he tossed the cigarette away.

****

Standing on Main Street, Gloria Knecht was observing the sky as well. When she spotted the same thing that Lasky – and probably many others – were seeing, she was in awe. Never in her hundred and seventy five years on earth had she witnessed anything quite like it.

Viewing it, she was troubled. In her youth, she had enjoyed hearing the Christmas story when her father and mother read it aloud from the family Bible. She had been a good Christian girl, but that single afternoon in Salem, Massachusetts, a hundred and fifty years ago, had changed her forever. She could no longer believe that there was a God, only in the powers of darkness and evil.

As the years rolled along, she believed this ever more fervently when she witnessed the way people treated each other. She had lived through every war America had been involved in since the Civil War. She saw how greedy the rich became, seeming to want it all, apparently not giving a damn about the starvation and financial disasters befalling so many people she knew and loved – for she found that she still could love, even during that one-month period at the end of each decade when she became the epitome of evil. She was looking forward to starting her life anew as a human. Even though it meant being susceptible to the many harms that could befall a human being, she wanted it badly.

Gloria watched the anomaly in the sky for a few more minutes, and then shrugged her shoulders. If God chose to play a role in either her life or her death, she certainly would have no control over that...

She shook the thought off, laughing aloud. "There is no God, Gloria."

Realizing that she had spoken the words quite loudly, she looked around, but the few people nearby didn't seem to have heard her.

****

Orders had gone out at the beginning of the week that no police officer would have Christmas Eve off. In addition, those who were on vacation were urgently requested to report to work for their normal shift.

National Guard troops from both the Bethlehem and Allentown barracks were mustered to serve a two-day stint, assisting police officers in their normal duties and whatever additional support might become necessary.

****

Brian Miller was called in to work because of a sick call from his sub. The mail flow was heavy, and management wanted every piece of first-class mail delivered, no matter what. Although the volume of parcels had decreased, each carrier was still handling enough to push them into overtime on a day when many of them would have preferred to get home early, to prepare for Christmas Eve services at their churches.

He hated when he had to work on Friday or Saturday of his three day weekend because with rotating day off, letter carriers only had one Saturday off every six weeks.

As he cased letters, Brian remembered his first Christmas Eve with the Postal Service. He had only been three weeks into his career, delivering mail in a residential community that consisted mainly of row homes. It was a walking route, and the mail he was to deliver was placed in relay boxes scattered along his path of travel.

Freezing rain had pelted him all day long and, since he was not yet authorized to wear a uniform, he had on a pair of jeans and boots. By noon, his hooded sweatshirt and windbreaker were saturated, chilling his body to the bone. The carrier who had brought Brian out to the route headed back to the post office at three-thirty. As a result, when Brian was finally finished, he had to call in for a ride back.

He got home about six-fifteen, took off his ice-covered jeans and stood them on the floor. Then he grabbed a hot shower, a quick bite to eat and quickly walked the two blocks to church just in time for the seven PM service.

After the service, he returned home, had a beer and was asleep before ten. When he awakened Christmas morning, he asked himself why the hell he wanted to be a mailman. In the end, however, the desire for a well-paying job superseded the numerous small but annoying reasons that bugged him about the work.

****

Jessie Sterling only had to work for a half day and she was looking forward to making a light dinner for herself and Brian before church. That made it all the more disappointing when Brian called and told her he would probably not be home until close to six PM, which meant that they would have to go to the late service.

Trying to stay positive, she decided to take a little nap, knowing that they would be out late.

****

Mike and Sara reported to work for the three-to-eleven shift. He wasn't happy about it, and he knew that his partner felt the same, but they had a job to do, especially if they hoped to assist in killing Gloria Knecht. Only when that had been accomplished could their lives, and the lives of many local people, get back to normal again.

Mike feared that the residents of Bethlehem and the large number of tourists would grow more agitated with each passing hour. Everyone knew that Gloria would have to claim her last victim by that night, but no one yet had a clue as to where she was or who she might choose to abduct and kill.

The first few hours of the shift passed calmly, with nothing out of the ordinary happening. Then Mike's cell phone rang.

He pulled over into an available parking space and answered.

"Mike? It's Brian Miller. I think Gloria is going to grab Jessie. I just came out from work and found two tires on my car slashed. Can you and Sara head over there right away?"

"Sure, Brian. Sara and I are on the way. We'll be passing by the Post Office, so we can pick you up. We should be there in five minutes. We're going to get a call out to the Hellertown police and have a unit get over to your place right away. Everything will be okay." He toggled the lights and siren.

"Please hurry, Mike. I'm worried sick. I've been trying to get her on the phone but she isn't answering. That's not like her."

"Okay, we'll be there very soon."

When Sara called the Hellertown Police Station just before she and Mike arrived at the Post Office, she told them that there was a possible abduction taking place in Society Hill. She gave the address and was informed that a car would be there in five minutes or so. She urged them to send out two units, one to go to Brian's house and the other to block the only road that led into the community, but there were no other units available.

Sara next contacted the state police and informed them of the situation and the locations to where the abducted woman might be taken. All available units were then contacted to respond to the area as quickly as possible.

****

After slashing Brian's tires, Gloria took a cab to Hellertown, to the corner of Main and Water Streets, and made her way on foot up Society Hill. Nestled in her purse was the key she had found hidden in a fake rock in the small shrubbery garden outside Brian's front door.

Reaching the address she sought, she walked to the back of the house, where she spotted lights on in the bedroom: probably Jessie, getting ready for her man to come home. Gloria strolled back around to the front of the house. Several neighbors across the street had their lights on, but she didn't see anyone at the windows.

Quickly, she unlocked the door and slipped inside.

****

With a screech of brakes, Mike and Sara arrived at the post office. As soon as Brian hopped into the car, almost before he closed the door, Mike started up again, driving as quickly and safely as he could. On the way, they listened to the radio traffic. While Brian was talking to Mike, Sara had called the station to request that the radio dispatcher alert all vehicle patrols to Gloria Knecht's possible presence in Hellertown. They were moving forward on the theory was that she planned to abduct Jessie Sterling and take her to one of the three places Lasky and Jack McGinnis had determined were the highest points overlooking the city. Each patrol car on the street knew where to go, and Sara heard the sounds of sirens coming through on the radio.

Travel had grown increasingly more difficult as the snow turned from light flurries into a full-blown storm. Three inches had fallen since noon, forcing Mike to drive more and more cautiously, costing them time.

****

Jessie heard footsteps approaching the bedroom. Had Brian gotten out of work earlier then he'd anticipated?

"Hi, honey," she called out. "I'm glad you're..."

Gloria Knecht walked into the bedroom.

Terrified, Jessie curled up, frozen in shock on the bed.

"Hi there, Jessie. Get dressed. You and I have a little business to take care of, over on South Mountain."

"I'm not going anywhere, you fucking bitch."

Gloria laughed in her face. "Sticks and stones and all that shit, kid." She grabbed Jessie by the hair, tossing her from the bed like a rag doll. "Don't fuck with me. I said get dressed, and I mean now," she ordered, flashing her fangs for emphasis.

As soon as Jessie was dressed, Gloria grabbed her arm and pulled her through the house. Jessie stumbled down the stairs, landing hard against the front door, but Gloria picked her up roughly and hauled her outside.

A siren wailed, growing louder by the instant.

Gloria opened the passenger door and tossed the groggy woman onto the passenger seat, pulling the seat belt tight with inhuman strength. Then she hopped behind the wheel, backed out and then shifted the SUV into first gear.

As she began moving forward, the cop car came around the corner. Gloria hit its driver's door just hard enough to push the car off the road and onto the sidewalk, where it stopped just short of hitting the lower condo unit.

She sped out of the community and hung a left down Water Street.

****

Mike had just crested the hill about a hundred feet from the Society Hill entrance when he spotted a silver Subaru Forester pulling out onto the street and make a left turn.

"Mike, that's Jessie's car. Follow it!"

The two cars raced on the slippery street all the way out to 378. The traffic signal was red, but Gloria didn't hesitate. She turned right, sideswiping a blue Toyota. A chain reaction of six cars hit one another as Jessie's car started up the hill, with Mike less than five car lengths behind.

When they reached the top of the hill, Jessie's car skidded into a right-hand turn. Clearly, Gloria and Jessie were heading to the Star of Bethlehem. Sara quickly called it in. By the time the Forrester pulled up to the Star, three Bethlehem cop cars and two State Police vehicles were only a few minutes away. Detective Lasky, monitoring all the calls, was also on the way up to South Mountain.

****

Gloria hopped out of the car and raced to the passenger side, where she tore the seat belt from its housing and pulled Jessie out. Half dragging her, she arrived at the gated attraction and broke the lock, yanking the gate nearly off its hinges.

Noticing shadowy figures in the woods, she pulled Jessie to her feet. "Stay back or the woman dies!" she spat, baring fangs, as she wrapped an arm around Jessie's neck.

When Mike, Sara and Brian arrived, the snow stopped as quickly as it had begun. Even before the car had come to a complete stop, Sara jumped from the moving vehicle, drawing her weapon as she ran toward the bright lights. Brian and Mike followed her, running toward the Star.

They could hear sirens converging on the scene. Within two minutes, twelve cops and Detective Lasky and a half circle of law enforcement individuals with drawn weapons had Gloria Knecht and Jessie Sterling in their sites.

"Don't try anything stupid, people!" Gloria exclaimed, pulling Jessie even closer.

Jessie was now fully conscious, trying everything she could think of to break away from Gloria's grasp, without success.

Brian stepped closer. "Gloria, you don't really want to kill her. Let her go. Nothing will happen to you."

"Yeah, right, mailman! You think the minute I let her go, I'll be free?" She made a sweeping gesture with her other hand. "All you bastards would take potshots at me, even though you all know that bullets don't have any effect on me."

Brian got down on his knees. "I'm begging. Please don't kill her. Take me in her place."

"Mailman, that's so heroic of you, but you know I need the blood of a woman." She suddenly sniffed the air and smiled. "Of course, if Sara would be willing to trade places with her, I could honor your wish. How 'bout it, Sara! Are you willing to trade places with Jessie here? "

A couple of hours earlier, Sara had been startled to feel the cramping, exhaustion and wetness that accompanied a period. She hadn't had one for such a long time; she'd almost forgotten what it felt like. She tossed her gun to the ground and walked toward Gloria, still harboring a hope that one of the archers hidden in the trees would be able to take a shot.

Gloria grabbed Sara around the neck and released Jessie.

Jessie ran to Brian, sobbing as if she would never stop.

The archers had their bows drawn tight, the potentially lethal arrows ready to drive deeply in Gloria's heart and finally end both her reign of terror and her life.

Lasky cried out. "Why, Gloria? You know that even if you kill Sara, you won't get off this mountain alive."

"You want to know why? Alright, I'll tell you. It's a curse, Hyram, a witch's curse that changed me into a vampire, all those years ago. I have to drain Sara of her blood in order to break the curse once and for all. I'm going to get off this mountain alive and finally live as a normal human "

The sky was pitch black until, in one singular moment, the clouds parted to reveal the conjunction of Venus and Jupiter, forming a horizontal line of light. A comet flashed in front of the two planets, its tail creating a cross in the night sky. A beam of light filtered downward, bathing Gloria and Sara in an eerie white light.

With Gloria's attention diverted upward, Sara managed to escape her human bond and dive to the ground.

Gloria knew her dream of becoming a human would end in moments. Resigned to her fate, she stood as tall and proud as she could; spreading her arms to offer a target for whatever came her way.

Jack McGinnis and Joseph Begaye, a Native American, loosed their arrows. When the glass tips disintegrated upon contact with her breast bone, the filled shafts continued on, burying themselves deeply in her chest, spilling the holy water into her heart.

Gloria screamed and writhed as the holy water acted like a cancer, destroying the cells that formed the human heart. She scratched at her chest, bared her fangs and let loose another unearthly scream. Then she fell to the ground, dying

Lasky, Mike and Brian cautiously approached Gloria's convulsing body. As they watched her expire, a smile formed on her face, and the aging process rapidly turned her from a beautiful young woman to a leather-faced ancient, decomposing in front of their very eyes until nothing was left, save for the dusty imprint of a body on the surface of the earth.

Moments after she died, the comet disappeared as Venus and Jupiter began moving back toward their regular orbits.

Saturday, December 25th, 2010, Christmas Day

Brian Miller opened the balcony door and stepped outside. The morning air smelled more wonderful than any day he could remember.

Jessie had been deeply shaken by being held hostage and witnessing the destruction of Gloria Knecht. Brian had held her for a long time before she finally drifted off to sleep, nestled in his arms, her head on his chest. He hadn't dared to move for fear of disturbing her much-needed slumber. He was dead on his feet, having slept perhaps only an hour or so, but the hot coffee coursing through his body was beginning to work its magic. After two cups, he felt better and tiptoed to the bedroom to check on Jess, who was still sound asleep.

Brian fixed a couple of eggs and two slices of toast. He was still buttering the second slice when Jessie came into the living room, wearing nothing but his uniform shirt. He chuckled. "Honey, if there was one of you in each post office, I don't think anyone would retire. That shirt looks fantastic on you."

"Thanks, Brian." She grabbed a slice of his toast, sat down next to him and finished it in a quick flurry of bites. He handed her the plate and she finished everything else on it in short order, emitting an unladylike belch when she finished. "'Scuse me, Brian. I guess I was really hungry."

He rubbed her thigh. "How are you feeling this morning?"

She sighed. "Rested...but the image of Gloria is going to haunt me for a long time. I don't want to ever see anything like that again," she said, and began to sob.

He took her in his arms and rubbed her back until she calmed herself and leaned back against the sofa, breaking his hold. "It's hard to believe it is really over, isn't it?"

He nodded. "I thought that you and then Sara were going to die at her hands. I don't know what I would have done if I'd lost you. I want to be with you for the rest of our lives."

She smiled. "Brian Miller, is that a proposal of marriage, this soon after we became lovers?"

"Well, I didn't actually propose, but yes, Jessie Sterling, I'll marry you." He grinned, and found that his hunger had diminished.

When he stood up, he pulled her up by her arms, threw her over his shoulder, carried her to the bedroom, and then gently laid her down on the bed.

After they made love, they threw on robes and went out to the living room, handing each other presents from under the tree. When she opened the box containing the black diamond engagement ring, she smiled. Brian slipped it on her finger.

****

Mike and Sara spent the morning in bed. He made coffee, toasted a couple of bagels, spread a thin layer of cream cheese on the four halves and carried the breakfast to the bedroom, where Sara was sitting up, reading the newspaper.

Most of the news was related to the previous evening's vampire slaying, and Sara felt a little badly that so little was written about what the day was really about: celebrating the birth of Jesus Christ. Although there were references to the miraculous light that had appeared in the night sky, much as the original Star of Bethlehem guided the three wise men to the stable over two thousand years ago to offer gifts to Him, the newborn King, little else was said

Mike handed her a steaming cup of coffee as she continued reading, then began to munch on his bagel.

When Sara finished the article she was reading, she put the paper down and took a long sip of coffee, then looked at him, smiling brightly. "I'm so glad we are alive today and able to spend Christmas together. I never thought this would happen, but I'm happy to be with you now."

"I know, Sara. These past four weeks have really made me think about how lucky we are. We've got good jobs, and we've witnessed something that, with luck, will never be seen again. When she disintegrated before our eyes, I was spellbound. I've always believed in Jesus Christ and God, and I truly believe that, without Divine intervention, Gloria would have killed you and started up a new life as a human being somewhere else. I was so scared I'd lose you."

She nodded. "When she wrapped her arm around my neck, not giving anyone a clear shot, I thought it was all over. I never thought I'd be afraid of dying, but dying at the hands of a creature like her…" Her voice trailed off as she surrendered to her pent-up emotions, crying for a long time while Mike held her close.

****

Jack McGinnis and Joseph Begaye had celebrated their victory over the vampire with several hours of drinking, much to the dismay of Jack's mother. She had come home from the Christmas Eve service to find them acting like two lunatics, pouring beer all over themselves in her neat kitchen. But the world owed them a great debt of gratitude, and so she let it pass, and climbed the stairs to her bedroom.

****

Hyram Lasky was enjoying a cup of coffee and reading the paper, when his phone rang.

"Merry Christmas. Lasky residence."

As he listened to the caller carefully, his hands began to shake. Fumbling the receiver back into its cradle, he hurried to the bedroom, got dressed and was out the door in less than five minutes.

Twenty-five minutes later, he parked his car at the side of the road near a policeman. The cop walked him down a path through a thickly wooded area to a field where several police officers and Everett Gardner were staring at what appeared, from the distance, to be a large number of body parts. Hiram also saw a great deal of blood splashed over the snowy landscape.

He finally was close enough to see that there were three bodies, two men and a woman, ripped to shreds. Lasky felt bile rise in his throat, and he quickly turned away as vomit spewed from his mouth. When he recovered, he turned back to the bodies, then looked at Gardner. "What the hell happened here, Ev?

"I'm the one who discovered the bodies. After a quick examination, I called for some officers to help me transport them back the coroner's office. And then I called you."

Lasky saw that the officers were pale and there was evidence on their faces that they had lost their breakfasts, as well. He looked at Gardner again, his face ashen. "Vampires?"
Gardner slowly shook his head.

Hyram relaxed just a bit. "What then, Ev? Who could have done something like this?"

"Well, that's the thing, Hy. This wasn't done by any person or people. Look around and tell me what you see."

The detective looked the bodies over closely and saw definite bite marks. Body parts had been ripped from the bodies by something that possessed tremendous strength. Then he saw what Everett had wanted him to see, and he spewed again, then looked back at Everett, shaking his head.

"Yes, Hy. Those tracks are exactly what you think they are, even though there are none in Pennsylvania. And look at the size of them. I honestly believe these three people were attacked by one or more wolves – large wolves."

"Are you certain?"

"As certain as I can be at this stage, but after what we have all been through, I'm going to venture a guess that we are dealing with wolves with super strength, wolves that walk on their hind legs..."
You're not going to tell me...?"

"Walk with me."

They followed the wolf tracks a few hundred yards away from the bodies, where the imprints suddenly disappeared, replaced by the tracks of two barefooted humans.

Hyram Lasky dropped to his knees.

The vampire was dead. Now he and his men would have to find and kill two werewolves.

The End

About the Author

In 2010, Larry began work on The Christmas City Vampire as a National Novel Writing Month project. The object of the project was to write a 50,000 word seat-0f-your pants novel. He is very proud to have this book published by Bradley Publishings.

Larry has written three previous novels; 95 Bravo-published by www.writers-exchange in 2004, Requiem For A Vampire-published by Mundania Press in 2007, and Combat Boots dainty feet-Finding Love in Vietnam, published by www.lulu.com in 2009.

He is a Vietnam veteran and is the past president of the Lehigh Northampton Vietnam Veterans Memorial

He retired from the U.S. Postal Service in 2008 after working as a letter carrier for over 21 years.

Larry and his wife, Peggy, live in Hellertown, Pa., where he enjoys reading and writing. He has two grown children, Laura and Matthew.

In their spare time Larry and Peggy love to travel to the beaches on the East Coast. They have gone on two cruises and in 2003 had a dream trip to England and Scotland. In Scotland, Larry was thrilled to play golf at the St. Andrews complex.

Larry would like to thank his wife, Peggy for her total support.

He also thanks Saundra Julian for writing a great synopsis; Jim Rittenburg, Jon Choi and Nikolaj Christensen for their input. Special thanks to Billy Kounoupis, owner of Billy's Downtown Diner for making a cameo appearance in his book.

Larry would love to hear from you. Visit Larry Deibert's Books on Facebook, or send your comments to larrydeibert@hotmail.com.

Made in the USA
Columbia, SC
28 June 2017